Amber's Song

Also by Olivia, Camryn, and Kaitlyn Pitts

Ansley's Big Bake Off (Book 1—The Daniels Sisters Series)

Ashton's Dancing Dreams (Book 2—The Daniels Sisters Series)

And check out these titles by Alena Pitts!

The Lena in the Spotlight Series

Book 1—*Hello Stars*

Book 2—*Day Dreams and Movie Screens*

Book 3—*Shining Night*

Amber's Song

By Olivia, Camryn, and Kaitlyn Pitts

With Janel Rodriguez Ferrer

ZONDERKIDZ

Amber's Song
Copyright © 2021 by For Girls Like You

Requests for information should be addressed to:
Zonderkidz, *3900 Sparks Dr. SE, Grand Rapids, Michigan 49546*

ISBN 978-0-310-76963-7 (softcover)
ISBN 978-0-310-76964-4 (ebook)

Library of Congress Cataloging-in-Publication Data

Zondervan titles may be purchased in bulk for educational, business, fundraising, or sales promotional use. For information, please email SpecialMarkets@Zondervan.com.

Art direction: Diane Mielke
Interior illustrations: Lucy Truman
Interior design: Denise Froehlich

Printed in the United States of America

21 22 23 24 25 LSC 10 9 8 7 6 5 4 3 2 1

From Olivia:

To my mommy for always helping me find my happy place. And to all of my big sisters for being there for me.

From For Girls Like:

To our team for continuing to create, inspire and shape girls in the love of Jesus.

To our support family for being God's wind in our sails.

Chapter 1

"And there you go! *Voila!*" From her seat on the couch, my big sister, Lena, pronounced my hair done. "Take a look," she said. She passed her cell phone down to me.

I sat on the carpeted floor of my aunt's living room with my back to Lena. Taking the phone, I looked at the photo she'd snapped of the back of my head. Pretty braids covered my head in neat rows and flowed down my back.

I turned my head from side to side. "Wow!" I grinned. "Nice job, Lena."

Our Aunt Trini, who was sitting next to Lena on the couch, smiled proudly at both of us. "You're good with your hands, Lena. Maybe it's from all that guitar playing. It looks like you'll be an expert at braiding hair in no time."

Lena shook her head. "I only did okay because you were right next to me. Without you showing me what to do—or fixing my mistakes—her hair would never have come out this nice."

"Well, I *am* a professional hairstylist," Aunt Trini reminded her. "I have had years of experience. But that's why you should believe me when I say you did a good job."

"Okay," Lena said with a small smile.

Springing to my feet, I handed the phone back to Lena just as Aunt Trini gave me a hand mirror to look into. I checked my braids out again and flipped some with my free hand. "Even

1

though I'm *not* a professional," I said, "I think they look great too. Thanks, Lena! I really love them!"

"And while they're very pretty," Aunt Trini said, taking the mirror back from me, "they will also be practical for camp. The braids will keep your hair out of your face when you're doing sports. But remember what I told you about washing your hair and protecting it with conditioner before going into the pool."

"I will," I promised.

Aunt Trini sifted through my braids playfully. "And you can always tie them in a long—not to mention fabulous—ponytail when you want to."

"A 'fabulous ponytail!'" I laughed and jokingly did a small runway walk in front of the couch. I ended it with a toss of my head that flipped my braids behind my back. "Fabulous!"

I heard laughter from my other two sisters who were sitting on the other couch. I looked over at them. But something about the way they giggled made me know they weren't laughing at my goofing around. They were laughing about something else.

Then I saw the reason! Middle-sister Ansley and my twin, Ashton, were sitting side-by-side on the couch just like Lena and Aunt Trini were. Only they were weaving tiny, funny-looking braids into our dad's short, curly hair. They were also clipping pink, sparkly barrettes on the end of each braid. Dad didn't know. Because even though he was sitting on the floor, like I had been, his eyes were closed *and* he was taking slow, deep breaths. He had fallen asleep! I clapped both hands over my mouth and giggled.

Dad, my sisters, and I were all staying at Aunt Trinity's house in Texas for a few weeks that summer. She had spent a lot of our visit showing us sisters how to style each other's hair in different ways. We needed to learn because our mom knew lots of ways to style our hair but sadly she died last year. We really missed not having her around to love us and to teach us about God. But we also missed the smaller things she used to do—like our hair. Dad's sister, our aunt Samantha, lived with us now. And she did our hair most of the time when we were home in Tennessee. But since it was Aunt Trini who had first taught Mom how to do hair, she decided that she was going to teach us girls too. At least as much as she could during our visit. The braids on my father's head, though, made it look like some of us needed more practice!

Trying to be as quiet as possible, I waved in Lena's face, held a finger up to my lips, and pointed over at Dad. Lena and Aunt Trini both caught sight of his new hairdo just as the doorbell rang.

Dad's eyes flew open. He scrambled to his feet. "I'll get it," he mumbled.

We sisters squealed with laughter.

Aunt Trini stood up. "Um, wait, why don't I . . . ?"

But in a few long strides, Dad had already made it to the front door. "Hello, Gio!" we heard him say.

"Hi there . . . Mr. . . . Daniels," a familiar voice replied. The surprised quiver in her voice made it sound like she was trying not to laugh.

Ashton and I gasped. "Giovanna!" we said together and ran for the door.

Giovanna Rossi was an old friend of ours from when we used to live in Texas. Since we moved away right after our mother died, we hadn't seen her in person for a year. She had come to stay over at our aunt's house for the night so we could all get an early start to camp the next day. Dad was going to drive us all there.

When Ashton and I reached the front door, we saw Gio grinning widely as she stared up at our father's hairdo.

"Oh!" Dad brought a hand up to the top of his head and he began touching the barrettes. He burst out laughing. "As you can see, I just came from the salon."

"It's really you," Mrs. Rossi said in an amused voice.

"I like to stay on trend," Dad joked. "Come in, come in." He opened the door wider.

"Oh, is it okay if I don't? I have Mr. Rossi waiting in the car." Mrs. Rossi gestured behind her.

"No worries." Dad took Giovanna's trunk from her mother's hand. "Come on in, Gio."

After giving her mother a quick kiss and hug goodbye, Gio ran toward me and Ashton. She squealed. I squealed. Ashton squealed. Then we all took each other's hands, jumped up and down, and squealed some more.

When we stopped jumping and squealing, Gio panted. "I've missed you guys so much!"

"We've missed you too," I said, still holding her hands and swinging them back and forth. "Come on! We'll show you where you'll be sleeping."

We brought Gio to a little study on the ground floor that had a daybed with a pullout bed underneath it. "You can sleep on the top or the bottom, or on the inflatable mattress." Ashton pointed to the cardboard box that was leaning against the wall near the doorway. "It's just not inflated yet."

"It doesn't matter to me," Gio said, flopping herself down

on the floor. "I can sleep anywhere. Sleeping is like my hobby." She laughed.

It was true. Last year at camp, Gio was always the first to fall asleep, the last to wake up. Ashton usually fell asleep pretty easily too. I know because I was usually the last one to fall asleep. I didn't like the dark. And I couldn't sleep unless I kept a night-light on.

My night-light! Did I remember to pack it? I wondered. *I'd better check.* I had meant to bring my night-light from home. It was shaped like a little cat and gave off a warm, cheerful glow when it was plugged in. I hadn't checked to make sure I had packed it before because I hadn't needed it the past few days. Once Ashton and I were in bed, Aunt Trini always left our bedroom door open a crack and a dim light on in the hallway for us.

I dragged out my trunk from under a nearby desk and began to look through its compartments. *Hmm. Not in the front pocket . . . not in the side pocket . . . not in the* other *side pocket. Gosh, I hope I didn't leave it back home!* I felt my heart begin to thump fast. I unzipped the small pouch that held my toothbrush and toothpaste with shaking hands and began to search through it. No night-light. *Maybe it's somewhere under all my clothes.* I sighed deeply. The only way to make sure was to take out everything Aunt Sam had neatly packed *and* what I had *secretly* packed. I tried to hide what I was doing from Ashton, who was busy chatting with Gio, but it was impossible. I took out a stack of T-shirts, some pairs of shorts, some sneakers . . .

Ashton stopped talking to Gio and frowned. "What are you do—?" Then she let out a tiny gasp as she caught sight of something soft and white in my suitcase. "You packed your *kitty coat*? In the middle of *summer*?"

My "kitty coat" was a fluffy, white, fake-fur jacket that had been the last present my mother had given me. When it was new, I wore it practically every day and Mom started calling me her "fluffy little kitty" whenever she saw me with it on. She would even pet me by stroking my "fur" as I snuggled up against her. Soon "fluffy little kitty" got shortened to just "kitty." And it became Mom's special nickname for me. Nowadays "Kitty" was the nickname that my whole family called me privately at home.

"Yes . . ." I said. But seeing the look of disbelief on Ashton's face made my face burn. I turned away from her and suddenly noticed my cat night-light tucked in the side of the suitcase, protected by some rolled-up socks. Feeling a wave of relief pass over me, I snatched it up and gave it a little hug. Then I began covering up my kitty coat with the T-shirts and shorts I had just taken out of the suitcase.

"When do you think you're going to get the chance to wear it at camp?" Ashton went on. "Plus, it's going to get so dirty if you do!" She turned to Gio. "Can you believe that? She packed a coat for a Texas summer!" Then she turned back to me only to shake her head. "Did you already forget how ridiculously hot it gets here in the summertime?"

I felt my heart give a pang. I knew everything she said was right, but I didn't care. "But our cabins are air-conditioned," I said, still not looking at her. "You know how cool they can get. I can wear the coat like . . . a kind of robe."

From the corner of my eye, I could see Ashton shake her head again. "You should have just brought a robe then."

Even though we were twins, Ashton and I were not the identical kind. We didn't look alike and our personalities were quite different.

For instance, Ashton was more serious than me. She could also be very practical, which is why she didn't understand why I would want to bring my fluffy coat to camp. She probably even thought it was silly of me. (I could be silly sometimes! It made life more fun!) But I wasn't bringing the coat with me to be silly. It was just that sometimes wearing it made me feel like I was getting hugs from my mom. Plus, Mom had given me the coat more than a year ago. I had grown since then. And although I wasn't much bigger than I was the year before, I was taller than Ashton now—and even Ansley—so I had the feeling that it wouldn't be much longer before I grew out of my coat. I wanted to wear it every chance I could. Even if I had to sleep in it!

Suddenly Gio laughed. "I really *did* miss you guys!" she said. She tucked a lock of hair that had slipped out of her ponytail behind her ear as she looked back and forth from me to Ashton.

"We missed you too!" Ashton and I said together. We got on either side of her and hugged her.

"Twin cuddles!" Gio said. She wrapped an arm around each of us and gave us a squeeze.

When we broke apart, Gio jumped up and pointed to the small, curvy case that leaned against the wall near the door. "What is that? A tiny guitar or something?"

"It's a ukulele," I said. I snatched it up and brought it over to show her. After I unzipped the case, I showed it to her and plucked a few strings. "See?"

"So basically, yeah, a tiny guitar," Gio said, with a grin. She looked me over with wide and shining eyes. "I didn't know you could play!"

"Yeah, well, Lena's been teaching me."

"Maybe you'll get the chance to be a leader of song or

something," Gio said, running a finger lightly over the ukulele strings. The theme at camp this year was "All Creation Sings Praise," which, according to the brochure, meant that there would be singing classes as well as outdoor sports and nature activities. "You know," Gio continued as I put the uke back in the case, "since you got to sing that solo at the talent show."

I kind of wanted to just curl up in a blanket and hide when she said that. I mean, actually at *first* it felt like my heart grew wings and zoomed up my chest at her words. Part of me loved-loved-*loved* the idea of singing on stage. And wanted to do it again as soon as possible. But another part of me froze up inside at the very idea of having to perform in front of a lot of people. On the day of the school talent show that she mentioned, I had been so nervous I thought I was going to throw up before I sang! (I didn't.) What ended up helping me a lot was that Ashton was on stage with me that day. Although she didn't sing, she danced. But at least I hadn't been all alone up there. I just shrugged at Gio's suggestion. "Maybe." I put the ukulele back in the case and then on top of the desk. "I'm not bringing it with me. It's Lena's," I explained.

"Girls!" Aunt Trini called from the kitchen down the hall. "Anyone for some freshly popped popcorn?"

Gio, Ashton, and I all exchanged glances. 'Anyone'? Make that *all* of us! "Coming!" We all yelled together, and we ran out of the room.

Chapter 2

The next morning, before heading off to camp, we all ran around the house making sure we hadn't forgotten anything. We looked like blurs streaking through the rooms. And even though Lena was staying behind with Aunt Trini, she helped us get ready by helping with breakfast and carrying our bags to the minivan.

When Lena took my duffel, Ashton whispered to me, "I hope you remembered to leave your kitty coat here."

I said nothing. I just watched as Lena safely tucked my bag in the back of the van and I smiled a tiny smile. My coat was still inside of it.

After enjoying a noisy and excited breakfast and packing a lunch to eat on the road, we all stood in front of the car and formed a circle. Then, taking each other's hands, we closed our eyes and listened to Dad as he led us in prayer.

"Heavenly Father," he said, "thank you for this day and the opportunity to be a part of this adventure. We don't take your kindness for granted. We ask for your protection and your guidance as the girls head off for camp. Speak to their hearts, Holy Spirit, and use their time to grow them closer to you. In Jesus Name, Amen."

Then, as he settled into the driver's seat and went over a few last-minute things with Aunt Trini, Lena gestured for us girls to gather together.

"It's been a while since we've done this," she whispered to Ashton, Ansley, and me. "But since we are going to be separated for a little bit, I think it's a good time for it." She stuck out her right hand in the middle of the circle we had formed and began to say, "Even in times when we're apart . . ."

Ansley placed her hand on top of Lena's, Ashton placed her hand on top of Ansley's, and I placed my right hand on top of them all. Then we joined Lena in saying, "The Daniels sisters promise with all our hearts that we'll always be . . ." And we began to chant, "Together *Four*-ever! Together *Four*-ever! Together *Four*-ever! Together *Four*-ever!"

Then we broke our hands apart and cheered and hooted, "Woooooo!" as we jumped up and down.

Finally it was time to go!

Ansley, Ashton, Gio, and I all got in the back seats of the minivan and buckled in.

"I just want to make one stop before we get on the highway," Dad told us as he adjusted his rearview mirror.

"You need to get gas?" I guessed.

"Right." Dad chuckled. "Then make that two stops!"

So our first stop ended up being at the gas station. But the second one turned out to be at our favorite old donut shop! When he pulled up to the store we all cheered. And when he bought a dozen donuts we cheered again. When we set off on the road again, Dad gave us permission to each have a donut immediately if we wanted, and we cheered a third time.

"This is already the best road trip, ever," Giovanna said, taking a bite of her Boston cream donut. "Mmm."

I nodded but my mouth was too full of sprinkles and strawberry glaze to say anything out loud.

"How about a soundtrack for the trip?" Dad asked and suddenly the soundtrack to *The Winter Sisters*, a Broadway musical we had all seen a few weeks back on a trip to New York, filled the car.

Immediately my sisters and I began to sing along to "It's Time"—the song we were most obsessed with. We sang loudly and dramatically,

> *I know it's my time*
> *My time to step up.*
> *It's time to be heard.*
> *It's my time to speak out,*
> *Make you hear my words.*
> *This is my song . . .*

Dad groaned. "What did I do?"

And we all burst out laughing, knowing how we'd been driving him nuts for weeks singing that around the house. When the song was over, he switched over to some praise and worship music, and "God is Good" by Mallory Winston began to play.

I saw Ashton close her eyes and knew she was imagining the dance she had created for the song and was dancing it in her mind. I started to sing along to this song, too, only not as loudly as before, and all by myself.

"That sounded pretty," Giovanna said. She licked some icing off her fingertips. "Is that the song you sang in the talent show at your school?"

I nodded. Ashton had danced along to my singing, with our friend, Jasmyn, who was in a wheelchair. We had sent Gio a video of it and a lot of people had seen it online.

"Maybe you can sing that at camp." She began looking through a brochure that she found in the back pocket of the driver's seat. The words "Camp Caracara" were written across the front with a drawing of a caracara bird. "Sounds like we're going to get to do some singing," she said. "It says here that there will even be praise and worship karaoke!"

"Holy karaoke?" I said. My surprised voice came out in a squeak. Everyone in the car laughed.

"Holy karaoke!" Gio repeated, laughing some more. "I've got to remember to use that!"

Ansley took out a donut from the box and widened her eyes. "Holy karaoke! That's a lot of sprinkles!" she exclaimed. We all laughed again.

"Holy karaoke, these donuts sure are good!" I said, patting my stomach. More laughter filled the car. And we kept going like that until Dad said, "Holy karaoke! There sure are some silly girls in this car!" Which probably made us laugh the loudest.

I picked up the pamphlet from Gio's lap and looked through it. "Besides singing, what I'm really looking forward to doing," I admitted, "is riding a horse again."

"Me too," Gio said. "I loved the one I got to ride last year. Do you remember? He was a pinto named Jackson. He was so sweet! I got to feed him and everything. I hope I get him again."

I nodded. Jackson was what is called a "paint" horse. He was brown with white markings that looked like splashes of paint. He was named after Jackson Pollock, a famous artist who used to splash paint all over his canvases. "But you don't really get to choose which horse you get, you know," I reminded her. "They just give one to you."

Gio shrugged. "Maybe I can ask for him, anyway."

I hoped she was right. Last year I had gotten to ride a beautiful horse named Misty. She was a dapple gray horse, which meant that she was dark gray in some places, light gray in others, and even had little white dots scattered on her coat like a fawn. She really did look like she was made of mist, and was the prettiest horse I'd ever seen in real life.

When we finally arrived at camp, it was about noon. The sky was a clean, happy blue, which somehow made all the grass that covered the grounds and all the leaves on the trees look more brightly green. It was like nature itself was excited to see us. The camp counselors were, that's for sure. I say that because as Dad drove us into the campgrounds, our van was surrounded by them. They were all dressed in different colored T-shirts and they welcomed us by cheering and jumping up and down. They waved at us through the windows and held out their hands for high-fives. Dad rolled down the windows and Ansley stretched out her hand to high-five as many as she could before we passed them.

"Phew!" Ansley sat back with a grin as she wiped her forehead in pretend exhaustion. "Twenty in one blow!"

Soon it was time to say good-bye to Dad, and a young woman with long, dark, straight hair and brown skin took down our names and introduced herself to us. "My name is Sonia Dominguez, but everyone here calls me 'Sunny.' I'm glad the three of you are together," she said, meaning me, Ashton and Gio, since Ansley had already left us to check in with the older group. "You three are all assigned to the same cabin. Follow me!"

She led us to where a group of five other girls were standing. "These are the rest of the girls in your group—" she began, but got cut off when four out of the five girls screamed with joy and ran over to us. "Amber! Ashton! You came! You're back!"

I was almost knocked down by all the girls wanting to hug me at once.

"I can't believe you're here!" a tall girl wearing sports glasses said. "When you moved I thought we'd never see you again!"

I smiled at her. "It's great to see you, Kaydence!"

"Boy, have I missed you," a redheaded girl with freckles gave me a squeeze.

"I missed you, too, Tangie," I said, hugging her back.

"We're going to have so much fun!" twins Harmony and Heaven said at the same time, and they linked arms and danced around in a circle.

The fifth girl was the only girl I didn't know from camp last year. Her shoulder-length curly hair looked like it couldn't decide whether to be brown or blond. She stood away from the rest of us dressed in a purple, tie-dyed T-shirt that was so big it looked like a dress. What was weird was I caught her squinting at me like she needed glasses or something.

I looked back at Sunny, who was smiling down at me and the group hug Amber and I were in with the others. "Awww! Great reunion, you guys. Let's go. You're all in Corinthians!" A couple of other counselors came by to help us with our trunks and soon we were all headed toward our cabin.

All the cabins at Camp Caracara were named after books in the Bible. Ours was named after the two letters St. Paul wrote to the Corinthians. And since our cabin was really like two cabins in one (joined together by a large bathroom with lots of sinks, showers, and cubbies) one cabin had a sign over the door that read "1 CORINTHIANS" and the other cabin had a sign that said "2 CORINTHIANS."

When we entered the first cabin, just inside the entrance there was a poster on the wall that read:

> Love is patient, love is kind. It does not envy, it does not boast, it is not proud. It does not dishonor others, it is not self-seeking, it is not easily angered, it keeps no record of wrongs. Love does not delight in evil but rejoices with the truth. It always protects, always trusts, always hopes, always perseveres.
>
> —1 CORINTHIANS 13:4–7

I had always liked that scripture. One time, Dad, who is a pastor, told me that I could substitute the word "Love" with "God" because God is love. So I began rereading it to myself, "God is patient, God is kind . . ."

"This is your room," Sunny announced to me, Ashton, Gio, and Kaydence. "You can start settling in." She pointed to the trunks the other counselors had already hauled to our room.

"You can just leave that there," I told the counselor who had my trunk. She nodded and set it at the foot of the bunk bed I had chosen.

"The rest of you, follow me." Sunny led Tangie, Heaven, Harmony, and the new girl through the cubby section and shower room to the bedroom on the other side of the cabin.

"Ahhh," I said, with a little twirl. I was enjoying the air-conditioning. It felt great since it was so hot out.

Ashton lay down on the bottom bunk of one of the two sets of bunk beds and sighed in agreement. "So cool and refreshing!"

16

Gio threw herself on the bottom bunk of the other set of bunk beds. "Time for a nap!" she joked. She began pretending to snore.

I laughed and started to climb up the ladder to the bunk above Ashton. Suddenly a voice from the other room cried out, "NO!" making all of us jump.

I leapt off the ladder and took a peek into the next room. It was the girl in the purple T-shirt. "I am not sleeping on the other top bunk!" she yelled at Sunny. "I'll fall off!" She covered her eyes and ran straight into our room. I had to dodge out of the way.

"I'm sleeping here!" she said, pointing at the bed Gio was sitting on.

Gio crossed her arms. "No way. I can't sleep on the top bunk, either," she said firmly, "and I called dibs on this first."

I knew that wasn't true. Gio could sleep on anything and anywhere. But I didn't say anything.

The new girl burst into tears. "I want to go home!"

We all stared at her and then each other with wide eyes. I turned to Gio to see if she would change her mind, so I was surprised when I heard Ashton sigh. "Fine," she said. "*I'll* take the other top bunk in the next room."

I slumped my shoulders. My sister and I had bunk beds at home. She always slept in the bottom bunk beneath me. It was what I was used to. I waved sadly at her as she dragged her trunk over into the next room and the new girl sat down on the bottom bunk of my bed. She was all smiles now.

"Thank you, Ashton. That was kind of you," Sunny said as she dragged the new girl's trunk into the room and set it next to mine. "Better, Maxine?"

17

The new girl nodded and wiped her eyes. Not that they even looked wet. And, I noticed, *not even a thank you to Ashton or Sunny.*

"Okay, time to change into your swimsuits, girls. You have a swim test in fifteen minutes." Sunny clapped her hands. "Let's get moving."

I hurried over to my trunk, flipped it open, and began hurriedly looking through it for my swimsuit and my hair conditioner. I had to move my fluffy jacket to the side.

"What's *that*?" Maxine asked, suddenly at my side. Her trunk was right next to mine.

"My kitty coat," I said, not wanting to explain further. Then, finding my swimsuit, towel, and my plastic case of hair products—including the conditioner my aunt had given to me—I slammed my trunk shut. "I just need to do a quick soak of my hair," I told Sunny.

Sunny, who had hair that was a lot like mine, nodded with understanding. "You know where the showers are," she said. "Be quick, please."

I ran to the bathroom, soaked my braids in the shower, and quickly covered them in conditioner. I loved its sweet, coconut-y scent. The whole time, I could hear Sunny hurrying everyone up. "Time to start lining up!" she called out.

Gotta go, I told myself. I shot out of the bathroom and was about to step outside to join the others when I noticed that Maxine was still in the cabin. She was standing in the middle of the room, between the two sets of bunk beds, running her hands up and down the sleeves of my kitty coat. Which she was wearing.

Chapter 3

I began to shake a little. "What are you doing?" My voice came out in a squeak.

Maxine's face got so red she looked sunburned. "Just trying it on."

"Take it off!" I squeaked again. I had wanted to yell, but my throat felt dry and tight and I could hardly make a sound.

Maxine slowly and calmly slipped it off her shoulders. "I was just taking a look at it."

"Looking isn't the same as touching," I said, managing to get my voice to rise just a little bit louder than a whisper that time. I snatched the coat from her hands.

At that moment, Sunny came in the room. "Why aren't you girls lining up outside?"

I pointed at Maxine. "Ask her!"

"I just wanted to see what this fluffy thing was!" Maxine shrugged her shoulders like it was no big deal. "She called it a 'kitty.' I wanted to know why."

Sunny just looked confused. "I'm not sure what you're talking about. Just go put on your suit, Maxine! We need to go now!"

Maxine ducked her head and ran between us to the bathroom.

Sunny looked down at the fluffy white coat in my hands. "Is

that yours? Why did you bring such a warm jacket to a summer camp? In Texas?" she shook her head. "Put it away, please."

It *had* been *away*, I thought to myself as I headed back to my trunk. Once I was there, I slipped the jacket to the bottom of my trunk as best as I could, piled everything else on top of it, and snapped it shut.

Once we were outside and in line, I slid behind Ashton. "What happened?" she asked me.

I almost didn't want to tell her. She had told me not to take the kitty coat. But after swallowing hard, I told her everything.

"You brought the coat?" Ashton blinked in disbelief.

But Gio, who was standing in front of Ashton and listening to our conversation, gasped. "How dare she?"

Kaydence, who was standing behind me, leaned in. "Wait, what happened?"

I repeated what I had told Ashton. When I was done, Ashton, Kaydence, and Gio all turned to glare at Maxine, who was standing at the back of the line.

"Guys!" I hissed. "Don't stare at her like that."

"She needs to know she can't go looking through other people's stuff," Kaydence said. And she continued to glare, even when Gio and Ashton had stopped.

"You can keep the coat in my trunk if you want," Ashton told me as we began to follow Sunny to the pool.

"Thanks," I said.

The swim test was to see how well we could all swim (or not) so that the counselors could decide what swimming activities we were allowed to take part in. I could swim pretty well, so soon I was allowed to go down the huge waterslide and land on the giant pillow they had floating on top of the water. It had been one of my favorite swim activities last year. It was usually lots of fun to try to land as hard as you could to have other people who were already on the pillow bounce off and into the water. This year, though, I noticed Kaydence, Gio, and even Ashton all trying to land in a way that would bounce Maxine off.

It gave me a rumbly feeling in my stomach. I knew they were all doing it to get back at her for me, but it wasn't really something I wanted any of them to do.

"Guys . . ." I shook my head. "Don't do that, okay?"

But Kaydence just giggled. "We're just having fun."

When pool time was over, we all hurried back to our cabin to get changed for lunch. I rinsed out my braids and dried it with a T-shirt like my aunt had instructed. And even though I tried to avoid even looking at Maxine (since I was still angry at her) she came up behind me as we headed toward the main hall and asked, "So why do you call it a 'kitty coat'?"

"Because when I wear it I kind of look like a fluffy white cat. That's why people call me Kitty." I realized too late I should have said, "that's why my *family* calls me Kitty."

Because then Maxine said, "Oh! Should I call you Kitty then?"

I cringed a little. I didn't know how to say 'no.' But I also didn't want to say 'yes.' Instead I sniffed the air. "Doesn't that smell good? I'm hungry! Are you?"

We entered the main hall—which is called The Upper Room—together. The building sat on a little hill and was basically a huge cabin where everyone gathered for worship or meetings. It was also used as the cafeteria when it was time for breakfast, lunch, or dinner. My favorite use for it, though, was as a theater! As we followed Sunny to our table, I took a moment to imagine myself on the stage, singing in front of as many people that could fill the hall. It was a scary thought—but a thrilling one too!

"You look happy," a voice above me said.

"Huh?" I looked up into Sunny's face. She was grinning at me.

"It's just that you were smiling so wide," she said. "Are you happy to be back at camp?"

I nodded. "Uh-huh."

I was even happier when I saw that our group's table was so near the stage. As I sat down I noticed the fluttering hand of Ansley, who was waving to me and Ashton from her table across the room.

I waved back.

"Who's that?" Maxine asked immediately.

"That's my sister," I explained.

"How many sisters do you have?"

"Actually, I have three," I admitted. "One isn't here. Don't you have any sisters? Or brothers?"

Maxine opened her mouth to speak, but Kaydence spoke up first.

"I have two brothers, but they're too old for this camp now, thank goodness."

"Why are you glad about that?" Tangie asked.

"Because they're eating machines. If they were here, they'd eat everything in the kitchen before the week was over!"

We all giggled but I did a little more than the others. That's because since Kaydence was so tall and had brown hair, I figured that her brothers had brown hair, too, and that they were even taller than she was. So I imagined cartoon-character guys who were, like, eight feet tall and with mouths so big they could fit entire refrigerators into them—sideways!

"I'm serious!" Kaydence went on, even though she was laughing too. "The rest of us would have to go hungry for the last two days of camp!"

"My brothers are eating machines too," Tangie said.

And I immediately changed the brown hair of the cartoon-like brothers in my mind to red, like Tangie.

But then she said, "Only they're babies." And suddenly the picture changed to eight-foot redheads with hamster cheeks sitting in a double-stroller. This made me giggle even more.

Tangie just nodded at me. "They're only a year apart. I am serious, that's all they do. Eat and sleep. Well, and play."

"Camp would be perfect for them, then," Ashton said. "When they get old enough."

"Well, I don't have any brothers or sisters," Maxine said, cutting through our chatter. "Just servants."

We all stopped talking.

Maxine, seeing that she had all of our attention, went on, "Yes. I live in a mansion."

Uh-oh, I thought. I felt my stomach clench.

"It's on top of a hill," Maxine said, not really looking at any of us in the eye. Instead, she looked off into the distance, like she was seeing a vision or mirage of her house. Her voice got kind of dreamy. "And we have rolling green land surrounding us—more than you see here. And there are servants for everything. A butler who answers the door.

A cook. A housekeeper. I even have my *own* maid. She cleans my room and makes my bed . . . and runs my bubble bath . . . and brushes my hair . . ."

Ashton sighed loudly.

"You don't believe me," Maxine snapped out of her trance. I imagined her mirage disappearing with a poof!

Kaydence smirked. "Oh, it's not that she doesn't believe you. She was just wondering when you would get to the part where your maid walks your pet dragon."

We all burst out laughing at that. We couldn't help it.

Maxine's face scrunched up and she glared down at the table.

Just then, the director of the camp began speaking from the stage where she had gathered a bunch of camp counselors.

"Hello, everyone, your attention please. I'm Olive Cameron, the director of this camp, and I'm here to welcome you to another fun and amazing summer at Camp Caracara!"

The counselors all began jumping up and down and cheering, which inspired all of us kids to do it too.

"It is my hope that you'll all have a wonderful time during your stay here as we learn to appreciate and celebrate God's creation. That's why the theme this year is "All Creation Gives Praise!" We're going to go out and enjoy God's creation by playing in the sun and grass and admiring His handiwork. And we'll have fun creating stuff ourselves—especially using music. Because God wants us all to enjoy the fun of creating things too. So we'll have opportunities for you to make up songs, dances, skits, and works of art. And we'll be praising God through all of it. How does that sound?"

There were more cheers and clapping.

"Great! Because that's how it sounds to me too. Now, your counselors will be passing out your schedules, so you'll see just how you're going to spend the next week." With a nod she signaled counselors who were holding small stacks of green-colored paper to begin passing them out at each table. "And once you get those, you can look them over as we have lunch. I'm sure those delicious smells coming out of our kitchen have been driving you all a little crazy. But first, let's thank the Heavenly Father for bringing us all safely to another amazing summer at Camp Caracara!" Then, bowing down her head, she led us all in the camp prayer that was kind of like a school chant:

*"We thank you Lord for this day
to laugh and learn and rest and pray.
We thank you Lord for this week
to offer praise and wisdom seek.
We thank you Lord for this time
to swim and ride and hike and climb.
We thank you Lord for this year
to sing and dance and act and cheer!"*

And it ended with the room letting out a big cheer of "AMEN!!!!" and "WOOOOOO!"

As Sunny handed us our schedules, she said, "This was printed on one hundred percent recycled paper."

"Neat!" Heaven said, taking some and passing the sheets around the table.

I quickly scanned the list. The thing I wanted most to check was when I would get to ride a horse again. "Tomorrow!" I said out loud and I let out a squeal.

"What's tomorrow?" Maxine asked, craning her neck to look at my schedule.

"We're riding horses," I said, pointing. I knew since we were in the same cabin that her schedule was going to be the same as mine.

Gio, who was sitting on my other side, grabbed my arm and squealed too. "I can't wait! I hope we get Jackson and Misty again!"

Maxine squinted. "Jackson and Misty?"

"She means the horses we rode last year," I said, trying to sound casual. "You know, since we know them already."

"Oh. I have lots of horses at home," Maxine said in a dull voice, and she looked over her schedule with a bored expression on her face.

"How many?" Kaydence asked. "Ten? Twenty? One hundred?"

Heaven and Harmony snickered behind their sheets of paper.

But Maxine didn't flinch at Kaydence's words this time. "No! Don't be silly. We only have five. But one's a prize-winning race-horse. A thoroughbred."

"What's his name?" Gio asked.

"Rosetta Blues," Maxine said immediately.

I was surprised. The name sounded familiar. Like maybe it was a real racehorse. I looked at Gio to see her reaction.

She crossed her arms. Then she blurted, "You are *so* lying."

"I am not!" Maxine huffed.

"Too bad we aren't allowed cell phones. Otherwise we could look it up and prove it," Kaydence said.

"Yeah, prove that I'm telling the truth," Maxine insisted.

The girls glared at one another across the table.

Sunny, who had been talking to another counselor and missed what had just been said at the table, gestured for us to get up. "Time to get your lunch!" she said. "It looks good too!"

We jumped out of our chairs and headed for the buffet line. I was glad to get away from the uncomfortable situation at the table. Once in line, I got a tray and reached for some juicy strawberries to put on my plate when a voice in my ear made me jump. It was Maxine, who I hadn't noticed come up behind me, "And that's the name of one of my other horses!" she said.

I dropped the serving spoon I had grabbed to scoop up the strawberries. "What?"

"Strawberry. I have a horse named Strawberry."

"Oh," I said. "That's nice."

"Yes, and the others are Cinnamon, Sugar, Buttermilk . . ."

Was she talking about horses or pancakes? I wondered as I moved down the line and she followed.

"And my favorite, Priscilla. She's an Arabian."

"Uh-huh," I said. I put some cantaloupe on my plate. "Want some?"

Maxine shook her head. "And nobody rides Priscilla but me, she's all mine," she went on.

"Oh, okay," I said, to show her I was listening, but not because I thought what she was telling me was okay. In fact, I didn't think it was okay at all. What I really thought was *Ugh, just great. It looks like I'm going to have to spend the next week living with and listening to a non-stop liar!*

Chapter 4

After lunch we all got to go back to our cabins. Sunny told us to finish unpacking and then to join her at the picnic table on the patio.

"Okay, guys," Sunny said as we all gathered at the table. It was nice to sit out on the deck and be surrounded by grass and trees in all directions. "This will be a sort of 'getting to know you' exercise. You're all going to write 'I Am' poems."

"What's an 'I Am' poem?" I asked.

"It's a poem about yourself inspired by the fact that you are made in God's image. For instance. Do you know God's name?"

"You mean it isn't 'God'?" Tangie asked.

"No, that's really more like his title," Sunny said.

"Jesus!" Heaven said.

"Yes, that is the name above all other names. But that's the name of God the Son. I'm talking about the name of God the Father, Son, and Holy Spirit. Um, here's a hint: he told his name to Moses."

The picture of Moses bowing before the burning bush sprang to my mind. I scrunched up my face. "You mean, 'I Am,' right? He told Moses that his name was 'I Am!'"

"Kind of weird for a name," Maxine said, wrinkling her nose.

"It's not the sort of name you're used to hearing." Sunny nodded. "It's more like what his name means. All of our names have meanings. Like mine, Sonia, means 'wise.' Do any of you know the meaning of *your* names?"

"Mine just means 'heaven,'" Heaven said, laughing.

"And mine means 'harmony,'" Harmony joined in and laughed too.

"And mine means amber," I said, "like the gem. Hey! God's name is sort of in my name. I. Am . . . ber!"

"How cute! And how blessed you are!" Sunny said. "But getting back to—"

"Wait! What does my name mean?" Maxine asked.

"Well, think about it, Maxine. With 'max' in it and everything. You know what it means to 'maximize' something, right?"

"That's when you make something really big, right?"

"Yes. The biggest. Or the greatest."

Maxine smiled to herself. "I'm the greatest," she said to herself.

Kaydence rolled her eyes.

"Well, the true greatest one of all is God," Sunny said.

"Then that means I'm kind of named after him too," Maxine said smugly. "Like Amber!"

"You could say that," Sunny agreed. "But to go back to Scripture, God's name is 'I Am' because he is ever-present and everlasting. His name doesn't mean 'I once was' or 'I will be.' He has always been here since the beginning of time and always will be through eternity. He is *always.*"

"Isn't he also 'love,' though?" Ashton asked.

"Yes," Sunny nodded. "God is love. But don't forget, love is also eternal. God made us with love because he loves with an everlasting love. He wants us to love him and to love one another. That's the whole point of life! So, on that note . . ." she handed out some sheets of paper and some pencils. "Here is the format for your 'I Am' poems. And don't worry, they don't need to rhyme."

I looked over the sheet and read:

I AM

I am (Name one or two things that describe you.)
I hear (Could be what you actually hear or something
    from your imagination.)
I wonder (What do you wonder?)
I hope (What do you hope?)
I dream (Do you have any wishes? Ambitions? Real or
    impossible!)
I am (You can repeat the first line or think of
    something new.)
I see (Something you see with your eyes OR with
    your mind!)
I touch (What can you touch with your fingers or your
    spirit?)
I feel (What emotions are you feeling right now?)
I want (Is there something you want more than anything
    else? Anything you want right now?)
I am (Again, you can repeat the first or second line or
    make up a new thing.)
I try (Are you making any special effort to learn anything?)
I worry (Is there anything you are concerned about?)
I pray (What or whom do you pray for?)
I know (What is something you know for sure?)
I am (You can repeat the first line or choose
    something else.)

As I read it over, I knew exactly what I would write on the first line. It was from my favorite Scripture, Psalm 139:14. I had a framed copy of the verse written in my mother's handwriting, hanging on my bedroom wall back home. I bent over my sheet of paper and after the words "I am" I wrote:

fearfully and wonderfully made

"Um, don't worry about what your neighbor is writing," Sunny said.

I looked up to see who she was talking to. That's when I noticed Maxine quickly turn her head away from me. Had she been trying to copy me?

I scooted on the bench to put more space between us.

It took a while, but after twirling my pencil like a baton, tapping my forehead with its eraser, swinging my legs back and forth, and scribbling and erasing a lot, I came up with this poem:

I am fearfully and wonderfully made
I hear music and have to sing
I wonder where it will take me
I hope to be on Broadway one day
I dream of being on the stage
I am God's girl
I see the many gifts God has given me
I touch them one by one and give thanks
I feel grateful for all of them
I want God to know this
I am made from love
I try to be gentle and kind

I worry that I am not always
I pray for help to do better
I know God is always with me
I am made in the image of I am.

We were all quietly writing for a while when Kaydence asked, "Are we supposed to read these out loud?"

Some of the girls looked up from their writing with expressions of horror or panic on their faces.

"Only those of you who want to share," Sunny said. "You don't have to if you don't want to."

I raised my head and smiled at my counselor. I wanted to read my poem because I liked it so much, but I also felt too shy to raise my hand to tell her so.

She caught my eye. "Are you done, Amber? Would you like to read yours?"

I nodded and then looked down at my sheet of paper. "I am fearfully and wonderfully made," I began. Then I giggled nervously. "That's from the Bible," I admitted. "One of my favorite verses."

Sunny nodded encouragingly.

I went on. When I got to "I am God's girl," I explained, "That's what Mom used to tell me and my sisters. That we're 'God's girls.'" And when I got to the part about being made from love, I pointed to the cabin door. "Because we said God is love. And you know, there was that poster inside that said 'Love is patient, love is kind . . .'" Finally, I got to the end. "And since God made us all in his image and his name is 'I Am' that means I am made in the image of I Am. That is, we all are . . ." I trailed off and stopped speaking as everyone around the table broke out in applause.

"Nice job, Amber! I mean it! That poem turned out great!"

I shared a secret smile with Ashton. "My sisters and I all like to write."

"But you also read it out loud really well. Not everyone can do that. But if you want to be on Broadway that is a good skill to have. Maybe you'll want to read your poem out loud at Cabin Fever Cabaret Night on the last night of camp?"

"What's a 'cah-bah-ray'?"

"You remember from last year, don't you? At dinnertime on our last night, we have songs, skits, recitations, dance . . . all kinds of arts and entertainment."

"You mean sort of like a talent show?"

"Sort of. That's a good comparison, actually. It's not a competition, of course, and all the songs, poems, and skits will be about loving God, but yes. That's why I think your poem would be perfect for it. Maybe you could do something with it. Like a spoken word performance."

I didn't know what to say. I just giggled at the thought.

"You seem a little shy about it," Sunny said. Sunlight shone directly onto her face then, so she squinted as she smiled. "Well, think about it and let me know. Maybe some of you other girls would like to take part in a spoken word performance. Is anyone else interested?"

Kaydence and Gio said that they were. Heaven and Harmony said they *might*. Tangie said she hadn't even finished her poem yet, and Ashton said she wasn't really interested. When she was asked, Maxine shook her head 'no' and slipped her poem off the table and onto her lap, which surprised me a little. I guess I just didn't expect a girl who made up stories about having

34

horses and servants and living in a mansion to be shy about performing on a stage.

As Harmony started reading her poem aloud, my mind wandered back to the idea of performing at the cabaret. I really did think it would be fun. But the whole idea seemed extra scary because I would be reading—or reciting—my *own* words out loud, instead of someone else's. I mean, Ashton and I liked to write little skits and film mini movies on our cell phones. (In fact, it's really what we used our cell phones for: making movies—or taking photos.) And so of course, we wrote our own lines for them and performed them. But this would be different. It would be in front of an actual audience.

Remembering the stage I'd seen in the dining hall, I tried to picture myself standing on it, holding my poem in my hand. I saw my hands shaking, rustling the sheet of paper loudly into the microphone. Then I imagined the speakers letting out one of those loud, high-pitched feedback sounds—the kind that hurts your eardrums—and I saw everyone covering their ears and making faces. Finally, I saw myself opening my mouth to read the first line of my poem only to have my voice come out in a squeak—like it did earlier when I saw Maxine trying on my jacket without my permission. Sometimes when I'm nervous or upset it's what happens to me. My throat feels squeezed and it's like suddenly someone somehow lowered the volume on my voice. I sighed to myself. Oh, I would probably enjoy Cabin Fever Cabaret Night—only from my chair, sitting with the rest of the audience.

35

That evening, as we got ready for bed, I dragged my trunk out from under the bed to put my poem inside. Maxine, who was lying on top of the bed watched me closely as I folded the sheet of paper and slipped it into an inside pocket. Then I noticed a part of my jacket was sticking out under the pile of clothes that was on top of it. *I'd better give it to Ashton to look after,* I thought, remembering her offer.

"Ashton!" I called out. When she took the jacket, Ashton held it in a bundle in her arms. It made Maxine laugh. "It really *does* look like a kitty!" she said. "Hey! Where is she taking it?"

"To my room," Ashton answered firmly, "I'm going to lock it in my trunk." And as she returned to her room, I heard Tangie's voice coo in surprise. "Oooh! What's *that*?"

Maxine stared off into Ashton's room with longing. "Why did you let her take it with her?"

I said nothing. I was just glad that my jacket was now really hidden from her sight. And I was about to close my trunk when I found my night-light. *Oh, I almost forgot!* I thought.

"Is it okay with everyone if I plug in this night-light here?" I asked loudly. The socket was in the wall in the bathroom. I figured that way it wouldn't really be in anyone's way, and it would still bring a little light into our room.

Most of the other girls shouted out that it was okay.

"Sure!"

"No problem!"

"Oh, good, I don't like it pitch black either!"

But not Maxine. She grumbled, "That light is going to keep me up all night!"

"Why?" Kaydence asked. "Do you sleep with your eyes open?"

Maxine clucked her tongue.

36

"Besides," Gio added, "if it bothers you so much you can go to sleep in the other room like you were supposed to."

I saw Maxine cross her arms as I climbed into the bunk above her. "You can see it just as much from over there!" she said.

"Then close your eyes!" Gio sounded like a tired mom. "And just go to sleep!"

"I will," Maxine said. Her voice sounded like she was pouting. "I'll make believe I'm back at home, in my canopy bed. It's as big as three of these bunk beds lined up together. It's so cozy, when I'm there I like to pretend that I'm sleeping inside a pink cloud."

"You're right," Kaydence muttered into her pillow, "you like to pretend!"

"All right, girls!" Sunny called out from her bed. It was next to the bathroom, in the little walkway that joined our bedrooms together. That way she could look in at all of us. "Remember the Bible verse this cabin is named for. We are all supposed to be patient and kind! Time to get some sleep. Remember, we have horses in the morning!"

"Yay!" we cheered from our beds.

Now I'm *going to have trouble sleeping,* I thought as I snuggled down. *But only because I'm excited to go horseback riding again—and especially to see Misty!*

Chapter 5

"Rise and shine!" Sunny called out the next morning. "Let's praise the Lord for a beautiful morning and get ready to rejoice and be glad in this day that he has made!"

Misty! Here I come! I thought, as I sat up in bed. I looked down to give Gio a shared look that said, "Horses!" But her eyes were still closed even though she was smiling. I watched as she pulled her sheet over her head and turned to face the wall. She was not a morning person.

I hurried down the ladder, but Maxine still got to the bathroom before me. And right before I reached her, I saw her unplug my kittycat night-light from the wall.

"Um, that's mine," I said, thrusting out my hand so she could hand it over.

"I know." She turned it over and inspected it carefully. "It's a cat. I get it. Because you're Kitty." She dropped it in my palm and entered the bathroom.

She brushed her teeth very quickly and left before I had finished brushing mine. Then when I was done, before I put my toothbrush back in its place, I held it up to my mouth like a microphone. "I am fearfully and wonderfully made . . ." I whispered into it.

Just then, Ashton entered the bathroom from the other side and sleepily walked up to the sink next to me. "Are you using that toothbrush as a microphone?" she asked bluntly. Her deep voice was even deeper in the mornings.

I felt a little warm in the face. Then I decided to make a joke out of it. "I know it's my time, my time to step up, it's time to be heard . . . !"

And suddenly the whole cabin was rocking out, singing "It's Time" from *The Winter Sisters* at the top of our lungs. "It's my time to speak out, make you hear my word . . !"

Even Sunny joined in, only she changed the words, singing, "It's our time to eat now! Let's go have some food!"

This made us all laugh, of course. I was glad that Sunny liked to get silly sometimes—like me!

"Hey, I know!" Gio said (she had gotten out of bed when she heard us start singing). "Let's have a Winter Sisters concert here in our cabin during free time this afternoon!"

"Yeah!" We all agreed. That was going to be fun!

When we got to the cafeteria there were all sorts of delicious smells filling the air. Fresh juice and bacon and syrup—not to mention all the baked goods fresh out of the oven, like blueberry muffins. I closed my eyes and took in a deep breath. Then my eyes popped open. "I think I smell cinnamon rolls!" I told my twin.

Ashton scanned the buffet tables for them. "There they are! Oooooh! Yum! I hope they're as good as Ansley's!" Our big sister was a great baker. And we all *loved* her cinnamon rolls.

If they are half as good as Ansley's they will still be good, I decided as our table joined the food line. Only a part of me wished that Ansley had actually made them herself, even if it meant she had to get up at five o'clock in the morning to help out in the kitchen.

One table was filled with containers of milk and juice and bowls of fruit. I almost walked by the sliced apples when I suddenly remembered that horses liked them as treats. I grabbed a napkin and loaded it up with some nice-looking slices. Then I wrapped them up and slipped the bundle into the pocket of my shorts. I was going to give Misty a little present when I saw her later.

Once everyone was seated and eating, the head of the camp, Olive, stood on the stage as she had the night before. "We're going to start our day with a reading from the Word of God," she said. "This is from Paul's first letter to the Corinthians."

"Yaaaaaay!" My table broke out into a cheer. Then Kaydence got us chanting, "Corinthians! Corinthians! Corinthians!" But the word got too long to chant, and we started shortening it to "Cories! Cories! Cories!"

Ms. Olive looked over at us and smiled. "Maybe someone from Cabin Corinthians would like to read it for us?"

Sunny nudged me. "Why don't *you*, Amber?"

"Uh . . ." I said.

My table began to clap for me in a beat. "Am-ber! Am-ber! Am-ber!"

I swallowed hard. I didn't see how I could say no. "Okay."

I walked up to the stage and stood at the microphone. As I looked out at the huge room filled with every camper and counselor at camp, I suddenly had a flashback to the scene I had imagined yesterday. I felt tiny drops of sweat begin to form on my forehead as I looked down at the sheet I was holding in my trembling hands. I cleared my throat, and immediately felt sorry that I hadn't had any juice yet. My tongue felt fat and sandpapery in my mouth. Then I felt Ms. Olive put one hand on my shoulder (which helped to stop my shaking) as she adjusted the microphone with her other hand. She pointed to the place on the sheet where I was supposed to start reading.

"Right there, sweetie," she said in a low voice.

I looked.

Love is patient, love is kind.

It was the same reading from the poster in our cabin! The verses I loved and knew so well!

I didn't even know I had been holding my breath until I let it all out in my relief. Then, straightening my shoulders and clearing my throat again, I began—not even looking at the paper, but at everyone in the room, "Love is patient, Love is kind . . . "

When I was done, Ms. Olive patted my shoulder. "That was perfect!" Then she bent down and whispered, "What's your name?"

I told her.

She straightened up and said, "Everyone please give Amber Daniels a hand!"

The room broke out into applause. (My table was the loudest.) I also saw Ansley stand up to cheer for me from her table near the back of the room. That made me smile.

When I sat down at my table again, I took a big gulp of orange juice as Ms. Olive spoke about the day we were going to have. She ended with, ". . . so like in the Scripture that Amber read so beautifully, we are all going to reflect God's loving kindness to one another while we have lots of fun today, right?"

The counselors led their tables in more cheers of agreement.

When we all got back to our breakfasts, Sunny turned to me, her dark brown eyes shining. "You did a great job up there!"

I smiled as I picked up a piece of bacon.

"What do you think of doing it again?"

I nodded as I bit off a piece.

"You know, with your poem at the cabaret?"

I froze.

Then, after quickly chewing and swallowing, I giggled. (Oh, why did I always have to giggle when I was nervous?) "Um, I'm not sure," I said.

"But your read so well . . ."

"It's not that . . ." my voice was dwindling down to a whisper again.

"Then what is it?"

I shrugged my shoulders and began swinging my feet back and forth.

"Okay," Sunny said sweetly. She didn't press me. Instead, she turned to Tangie, who was sitting on her other side and who had called her name.

Ashton, who was sitting on my other side, asked, "Why don't you want to do it? You sang at the talent show. You read on the stage just now. What's so different about reading the poem?"

I leaned in close to my sister's face so that I could whisper to her. "The difference is that the song I sang at the talent show was someone *else's* music. Someone *else's* lyrics. The reading from the Bible was, well, the *Word* of *God*. My poem is . . . well, something *I* wrote. *Me.* People might not think it's any good. I mean, they might not like it." I shuddered. "Plus, the poem is *about* me. It's . . . personal. It's not the same thing at all."

Ashton nodded with understanding but then turned back to her pancakes. "Then just tell Sunny 'no,' that's all. It's not a big deal. She won't mind."

I sank in my seat a little. I knew Ashton was right—Sunny

wouldn't mind. She wouldn't make me do anything I didn't want to do. At the same time I felt like I would be disappointing her if I *did* refuse. Plus, there was that other side of me that really loved being on that stage and wanted to be there as often as possible. In fact, I kind of couldn't wait to get on the stage again! I sighed. I was so confused!

But when Gio said, "Let's hurry up and finish! The horses are waiting for us!" I couldn't help perking up. *Maybe being out in the open air and riding on the back of a horse will help me to clear my head and figure out what I'm going to do*, I thought as I shoveled forkfuls of pancake into my mouth. *One thing's for sure. It'll be fun!*

When Sunny led us to the barn, we were all so excited we looked like a line of rabbits hopping behind her.

The barn was basically a big, open shed with horses lined up on either side, facing its wooden walls. Hearing the huffing sounds the horses made when they breathed out of their nostrils and the broom-like, swishy sound they made when they flicked their tails—not to mention the sound everyone's feet made while walking through the hay (like walking through pom-poms) was like music to my ears.

Most of the horses were ready to ride. That's because there were counselors stationed all around the barn getting them saddled up. I realized that they must have gotten up and eaten their breakfasts a lot earlier than we had just to get them ready for us.

I scanned the barn to see if I could find Misty. Then I gasped. There she was! About halfway down the right side of the barn.

Suddenly someone squeezed my arm. "What? What is it?" Maxine asked in a panicked voice.

I turned to look at her and noticed she stood half behind me, like she was trying to hide from the horses or something.

"What's what?"

"You went like this," she said, and she sucked in her breath.

"Oh, no, it's nothing. Nothing bad, I mean. It's just I saw the horse I rode last year."

"Oh," she said. Her eyes darted from one horse to another. As she stared, she began chewing her fingernails. She bit each finger one at a time: first her thumb, then her pointer finger, then her middle finger, ring finger, and finally her pinky. Then she started all over again from her thumb to her pinky. And again . . .

"Um," I said, kind of mesmerized by the ritual. "Are you . . . *nervous* or something?"

Maxine pulled her ring finger away from her teeth and hid her hand behind her back. "What? No!"

"Ooookay," I said. "I mean, it's okay to be nervous."

"Why would I be nervous?" Maxine asked in a voice that was higher than usual. "I have ten horses at home."

Now it was ten? "Um," I said again. But at that moment, the counselor in charge of the barn came out to greet us. "Hello, everyone," she said. "My name is Iris Tam, and I will be teaching you riding this morning. For some of you it will be your first time on a horse, for others this might be more of a review, but it's always good to review these things."

Maxine clucked her tongue. "Let's just get on a horse already!" she muttered under her breath.

Counselor Iris went on, "Counselor Trish and Counselor Gus

are going to be handing out helmets and helping you put them on as I go over some basics, like the parts of a saddle, how we tack a horse, and the proper way to sit and steer . . ."

I was really glad that she reviewed some of the basics since I could only remember some of the stuff that I had learned last year at camp. (I mean, I'd even forgotten that we had to wear helmets!) And when I strapped on the helmet I felt goosebumps run down my arms. It was official. I would finally be riding again!

Finally it was time for us to start getting on some horses. Counselors began leading them out of the barn and bringing them over to us, two at a time. Most of us used a mounting block—little portable wooden steps—to be able to get into the saddle. Some of the horse's backs were pretty high up for shorter people like me. But some of us just got a boost or a "leg up" to help us get on the horse.

When Counselor Iris brought out a brown horse with a white mane, Gio clapped her hands together and clasped them under her chin. Besides its mane, the horse had a white patch that ran down its shoulders and onto parts of his two front legs, and another white patch that ran down one of his hips. It really looked like two cans of paint had splashed him.

"Jackson!" Gio sighed.

Iris turned to look at her. "You've ridden Jax before?"

Gio gave out a tiny squeal.

"I'll take that as a yes." Iris laughed. "Then would you like to ride him again?"

"Oh, yes! Please!"

When Iris gestured for her to come over, Gio sort of tip-toed excitedly over and then gently stroked Jackson's nose. "Do you remember me?" she cooed.

45

Jackson's head bobbed up and down twice, like he was nodding. Iris laughed. "Well, that looks like a good sign! Okay. Let me give you a leg up."

As Iris did that, Trish led two more horses out of the barn: one was a red-brownish color from mane to tail. The other was a gorgeous gray that looked like a watercolor painting come to life.

"Misty!" I gushed. She really was the most beautiful horse. The way her gray color was as dark as a stormy sky in some places, more of a silvery shade in other areas, and cloud white in still others. Her long mane was also black, white, and shades of gray. I waved at her. Her tail swished. *She waved back!* I thought happily.

"I guess she knows you," the counselor said with a smile as she brought the two horses over to where Maxine and I were standing.

"Can I give her a treat?" I asked. "I brought some apple slices."

Misty's dark-tipped ears rotated at the sound of the words "treat" and "apple." She turned her head toward me and wiggled her lips.

"Oh! She wants them!" I said, reaching into my pocket.

"No, don't give it to her yet. Not while she's wearing a bridle. She's got that bit in her mouth. She shouldn't eat anything while that's in her mouth. You can give it to her afterwards, though." Trish turned towards Maxine. "And this here is Blessing."

Maxine's mouth was turned down at the corners. She looked from Misty to Blessing. "No! No way I'm riding *that* horse!" She turned and pointed at Misty. "I wanna ride *that* one!"

Chapter 6

W ell, actually," Counselor Trish nodded at me, "this girl was
going to—"

"NO!" Maxine wailed. Her yell made some of the horses
yank their heads up and whinny loudly.

"Don't raise your voice, you'll scare the horses," Counselor
Iris said, coming over. "What seems to be the problem?"

I knew what the problem was. Misty was a gorgeous horse.
Like something out of a painting. She looked fit for a princess.
Blessing was just sort of . . . plain. But that's not what Maxine said.

She crumpled up her face the same way she had in the
cabin when she didn't want to sleep in the upper bunk. "I miss
my horse, Priscilla!" she whined. "She looks sooooo much like
her!" She pointed to Misty again and began to make sobbing
sounds. "I *have* to ride her!" She then coughed dramatically.
"Pleeeeeeease!"

Everyone was looking over at us to see what would happen
next. Iris shook her head at Counselor Trish. "Just let her ride the
horse," she said, and she walked over to the next set of horses
that were being led out of the barn.

"But—" Trish looked over her shoulder to watch Iris walk
away. Then, with a sigh she turned to me with her eyebrows
slanted upwards. "Is it okay if she rides Misty? You can give
Misty that treat later."

To my surprise, I found that my arms were crossed (I didn't know when I had crossed them!) and I was gritting my teeth so hard that they were starting to hurt a little. I could see Maxine peeking at me from the corner of her eye.

She let out a few more gulping sobs. "I miss Priscilla soooooo much," she said.

I gave up. "Fine." *Love is patient . . .* I reminded myself even though I was still gritting my teeth, *love is kind . . .*

"Great, thanks so much," Trish said. "That is very good of you." Then she smiled at Maxine. "Okay, let me give you a boost up."

Maxine wiped her invisible tears and eagerly hurried over to Trish's side.

Counselor Iris came back to me. "Sorry about that," she whispered. "But we're supposed to be patient with each other, right?"

"I know," I said, nodding.

"But you've got yourself a special horse, here, with Blessing."

I sadly watched as Trish led Maxine—and Misty—away from me. "Um, sorry, what?"

"I said Blessing here is special. He has a secret. Want to see?"

I nodded, not really caring.

"Well, you know how horses can sometimes have a marking on their forehead or nose? They are usually in shapes that we call a blaze or a star or a snip. Now, Blessing doesn't look like he has any markings, does he? But look," Iris whispered. She lifted up the fetlock (his horsey bangs) and moved the crown of the bridle to show me the white mark near the top of his forehead. It was in a small, neat cross.

"Ooooh," I said. It had been completely hidden from sight before. It really was a perfectly shaped cross.

"See, a secret blessing! And he has no other mark on him. That's why he has that name!" Iris stroked the fetlock when she let it fall back over the cross. "Isn't that right, boy?" she cooed. Then she winked at me. "I guess God's blessing *you* since you get to ride him!"

"I guess He is!" I agreed as I reached for the saddle horn and got a leg up onto Blessing's back.

We rode for about forty minutes around the paddock (which was a large enclosed area for us to exercise the horses). Our horses followed each other in a line, sometimes we walked them in a circle, sometimes we walked them around objects, or over objects, like sticks lying on the ground. The whole time our counselors instructed us on what to do.

"Remember, everyone, straight lines, straight lines! The reigns should be two straight and even lines from your horse's mouth to your elbow. And we should be able to draw a straight line from your shoulder to your heel."

Trish told Gio, "No slouching! It's good to be a little relaxed. But sitting like a sack of potatoes puts more pressure on your horse's back. And it'll be harder to control the horse that way. Pull yourself up, curve your back a tiny bit."

"Okay," Gio said, immediately changing her position.

"Good," Trish nodded with approval. "Much better."

"Make sure your thumbs are up, honey," she told me as I went by her with Blessing. "Not sideways! You don't want your elbows to stick out. That also makes it harder to control the reigns."

"Oh, right," I said, and instantly changing my hand position.

"Great. You got it."

"Watch your feet, Ashton," Trish said. "The stirrups should

be on the balls of your feet. If you stick your feet too far in you might get your foot caught in there. We wouldn't want that."

Ashton nodded with a laugh. "No, we wouldn't!" she said, and corrected her position.

"Okay, that's too far in the other direction. Remember, stirrup in the middle of your foot, heels down. Yes! Just like that. Good job."

As our horses clopped on the soft earth, I looked at all my friends and the beautiful horses they were riding. Everyone was smiling their faces off. I almost didn't want to look at Maxine, though, because I was still upset at her for taking Misty away from me when she knew how much I wanted to ride her again. But it was like my eyes had minds of their own. They kept wanting to look over in her direction because, truthfully, I really wanted to look at Misty most of all. So, when I finally just let my eyes do what they wanted, I noticed Maxine was the only girl riding in the ring who wasn't smiling. She looked a little pale and her eyebrows were close together. I watched as she took one of her hands off the reigns to wipe sweat from her forehead. When she did that, she leaned forward a little bit, and wanting to hold on and keep her balance, she probably squeezed the horse with her knees. Suddenly Misty was trotting instead of walking, and making Maxine bounce hard in the saddle. Maxine looked like a glass bottle bobbing up and down in a rushing river.

"Slow her back down to a walk, Maxine!" Trish called, hurrying over to her side.

"I-am-try-ing!" Maxine managed to say between her rattling teeth. But she continued to bounce.

Trish took Misty by the reigns and instantly slowed her back down to a walk.

"I thought you said you had a horse?" Trish said to Maxine.

"I do," Maxine said.

"Then why didn't you slow her back down to a walk?"

"Because . . . I *wanted* to trot."

I turned to look at Kaydence, who was riding behind me on a black horse. Kaydence shook her head. "Liar," she mouthed.

I turned back to face the front.

"Then why were you bouncing around in the saddle like that, instead of posting?" Trish's voice was gentle but firm. Then she projected it so that everyone could hear, "Okay, people, when a horse trots, it's a one-two, one-two, one-two gait. If you lift yourself up and set yourself down in the saddle as it is happening, you won't be dribbled like a basketball by the horse. Or hurt your lower back, for that matter. Watch me. See, you can come up out of the saddle on the 'one' and go back down on the 'two.' The 'one' will be when your horse's outside leg moves forward . . ."

Soon the lesson was over. The counselors helped everyone off their horses as Counselor Iris praised everyone for doing so well. Then she told us, just as Maxine was sliding off Misty, "At our next lesson we'll get out of the paddock and do some riding out on the trail. How does that sound to everyone?"

Maxine's eyes grew wide and she stumbled as she landed on the ground.

"Are you all right?" Counselor Gus asked.

"Fine," Maxine said, wiping her hands on her shorts.

"Yes!" Gio said, pumping her fist in the air. "Did you hear that, Amber? Maybe we'll be able to do some cantering! Or galloping, even!"

I shook my head. "I don't think we'll be galloping!"

"That's too bad," Gio said, snapping her fingers in an "aw, shucks!" kind of way. "I've never galloped before. I would love to give it a try!"

"Yeah," Maxine said, "galloping is great! I've done it loads of times. On my racehorse too. Now *that's* fast!"

Gio put her hands on her hips. "Oh, really? Then if you know so much, why did you take this beginners class with us?"

"Because," Maxine unstrapped her helmet and shrugged, "we're supposed to do stuff with our cabinmates."

"Not all the time!" Gio said.

Walking away from their argument, I followed Gus and Misty into the barn. When he noticed me, he asked, "Can I help you?"

"Um, I wanted to give Misty a treat, but she's wearing her bit."

"Oh, okay, let me just take off the bridle and give her a halter instead." Gus took a pretty, aqua blue colored halter off a hook behind him as I took the bundle out of my pocket and unwrapped it. "Okay, now take those apple slices out of the napkin and put them on your open hand. Make the palm flat, like a dinner plate."

Misty gobbled up the apple slices super-fast. When she was done, she nuzzled and sniffed me to see if I had any more. It tickled. "Wow! She eats faster than our dogs!" I said. I gave her a few pats on the nose.

"She likes her apples." Gus grinned as he stroked her neck. "Don't you, girl?"

I saw a flash of red brown from the corner of my eye and turned to watch as Trish led Blessing into the barn. I looked at my empty, sticky hand, and my heart sank. I hadn't saved any apple for Blessing!

I hurried over to Trish, who was taking off his bridle. She saw me coming. "Hi, there," she said. "Wasn't Blessing a good boy?"

"He was, he really was," I said, feeling my lips tremble a bit. "But I don't have a treat to give him." I gave Blessing a few sad pats on the back. "I'm so sorry," I told him. "I wish I had something to give you. Hey! I know!" I raised my pointer finger to the ceiling. "I can grab some more apple from the cafeteria and come right back!"

Trish chuckled. "Isn't your group already going on to their next activity?" She pointed to my cabinmates lining up outside the barn. "Besides, breakfast is over, so there won't be any food out in the Upper Room again until lunchtime. Tell you what, if you want, you can come by during your free time and help us give the horses a bath. Check if it's all right with Sunny. You can bring a treat for Blessing then."

"Oooh, I'd love that! Can I bring a friend?" I was sure Gio would want to help with Jackson.

"Of course!"

Thrilled with the wonderful opportunity I hoped to be able to enjoy later (*Please God, let Sunny say 'yes!'* I thought), I practically skipped my way to the rest of the Cories.

"What are you so happy about?" Gio asked. She raised an eyebrow and smiled at me.

I grabbed her shoulders. "You're going to be happy in a minute too! Wait til you hear—!" But then I noticed that Maxine had turned around at the sound of my voice and was glancing over at the two of us. "Uh, on second thought, I'll tell you later," I said, slipping my hands from Gio's shoulders. "When we're alone."

"Good idea." Gio narrowed her eyes and glanced behind her. Maxine turned right around and faced forward again. As we followed Sunny to our next activity, Gio tugged my elbow to slow me down a bit. "I can't believe Maxine did that to you!" she hissed. "The way she stole your horse like that!"

My mind flashed back to the scene that Maxine had made to make sure that she got to ride Misty instead of me. My stomach tightened at the memory. Still, I felt the need to remind Gio, "Well, you know, Misty isn't really *my* horse."

"I know!" Gio said. "But still! I mean, Maxine knew you were looking forward to riding her. You know she did that on purpose! And it was so mean!"

Even though I was going to get the chance to see Misty later, I still felt myself getting angry at Maxine all over again. My breaths got short and hot when I remembered how Maxine had rejected poor Blessing too.

Kaydence, who had been walking in front of us, had obviously heard a bit of what we were saying. She walked a few steps backwards so that we could catch up to her. "Don't forget her 'crying.'" She tsked. "So fake."

Ooooh. The fake crying, I thought. I clenched my fists. *That was annoying!*

"Yeah," Gio said. "That settles it, guys." She leaned in as she dropped her voice to a whisper. "We're going to have to get back at Maxine."

Chapter 7

A chill ran down my back, snapping me out of my anger. "Uh . . ." I shook my head at both of them. "No, guys. We shouldn't do that. My mom always used to tell us to never take revenge. That vengeance belongs to God. It's in the Bible and everything."

"But isn't letting her get away with lying and stuff also wrong?" Kaydence asked. "Besides, we're not talking about revenge. It's more like . . . we just want to teach her a lesson. That's all."

Gio rubbed her hands together and grinned. "Yeah. Teach her a lesson."

That did not sound good.

Gio went on, "She needs to know she can't keep doing stuff like that to you. Remember how she took your coat too?"

That memory made me wince. But the memory of my mom's words was stronger. "Forget it, guys. I don't need you to do anything for me," I whispered. "Really. It's okay."

"Lying and stealing are not okay," Kaydence said. "That's in the Bible, *too,* you know."

"I know, but—" I stopped and looked around me. Sunny had just led us all to the huge, outdoor pool. The sounds of laughing, screeching, and splashing filled my ears and the smell of chlorine filled my nose! I had forgotten that "Pool Fun" was supposed to come after horseback riding today. I had meant to run over to the cabin and protect my hair first, with the conditioner from Aunt Trini, but that plan slipped my mind when I went to give Misty her treat. "Oh, no!"

Leaving Gio and Kaydence together, I weaved through the other bunkmates to get to Ashton. She was talking and joking with Heaven and Harmony when I interrupted her. "I forgot to do my hair thing!" I said. "Wanna go back to the cabin with me?"

"Nah," Ashton said. She whipped out a swim cap from her pocket. "I brought this. Didn't you bring yours?"

"No! That's back at the cabin too!"

"You'd better ask Sunny, then!" Ashton said, walking straight toward the pool. With a quick wave at me, she jumped in. Heaven and Harmony followed, dropping like two cannonballs close behind her.

I ran over to Sunny and explained about my hair problem.

Trying to keep her eyes on the girls who were already swimming, she barely looked at me when she said, "Okay, then, but be quick." As Tangie and Kaydence jumped in the water, she leaned back, but their splashes still sprayed her in the face. She blinked fast and wiped her eyes. "And take someone with you." I spun around to look for Gio, thinking, *Great! This will be the perfect time to tell her about bathing the horses later. No one else will be around!* But just when I spotted her, she held her nose and leapt into the pool with a squeal.

"*I'll* go with you," a voice said behind me.

I pressed my lips together before turning around. It was Maxine, of course.

"Make it quick," Sunny said again, as she dabbed at her face with a pink striped towel.

"Come on," I said, trying to hide the disappointed sound in my voice. I waved at Maxine to follow me.

When we got back to the cabin I rushed to the bathroom, grabbed my conditioner, and jumped in the shower in my swimsuit.

"You did that yesterday," Maxine said. "Why do you do it?"

"To protect my braids from the water," I said scrunching up my face and running my head under the showerhead.

My eyes were closed but I could imagine the confused look on Maxine's face when she said, "To protect your hair from *water* you . . . get it *wet*? That doesn't make any sense!"

"Sure it does," I said, letting my hair soak in as much water as I thought it could absorb. "I get it wet with *fresh* water and seal it with conditioner. Since my head has already absorbed all this water, it won't have much room to soak up anymore. The conditioner coats my braids like armor or a shield. I use it to block out the chlorinated water. The chemicals damage my hair and make it real frizzy."

"Oh. So, it's like, science."

"Yeah," I laughed. "It's basically science."

"My hair gets frizzy in the pool too," Maxine said.

As I started plastering my braids with conditioner, I looked at Maxine with new eyes. It was true. She had curly hair that was already getting frizzy because she hadn't used a swim cap or anything the day before. "I guess it does," I admitted.

"Can I use some of this stuff?" She took the conditioner right out of my hand.

You don't have to be so grabby, I thought, and I opened my mouth to say it, but couldn't get myself to. Instead, I said, "Um, it's just conditioner. Don't you have any?"

I didn't finish speaking before she was glopping a handful on her hair.

I grabbed the conditioner back. "Don't use it all!" I said, suddenly feeling a little panicked. "I have to share with Ashton!" And I didn't even bother to tell her she was doing it all wrong, because she hadn't even saturated her hair with water first. "You don't even need that much . . ." I sighed, but inside I felt myself filling with anger. Why did she always have to take things that weren't hers? And without asking first?

"Come on," I said, shutting off the water. "We need to go."

I slammed the conditioner down on the sink and marched out of the cabin, leaving her to follow me.

"Wait up, Amber!" she called out.

But I sped ahead and reached the pool before her. I didn't even check to see if she was still behind me before I jumped in and swam over to Kaydence and Gio.

"So," Gio said, slicking down her hair. "Kaydence and I have a plan."

"Not a big one. Just a 'for now' one," Kaydence said with a shrug.

"What? What is it?" I asked. We were all waving our arms and churning our legs underwater while having our conversation.

But suddenly both of them were staring over my shoulders. "Here she comes," Gio said.

Just as I began to look behind me, both Gio and Kaydence screamed, "Shark!! SHARK!!" and began swimming away at full speed.

"Come on, Amber!" Gio screeched. "Don't let the shark get you!"

I couldn't help it. I laughed. Then, I swam after them shouting, "Shark! Shark!" too.

When we were half a pool away from Maxine, we stopped in place again and cracked up together. "That was your plan? To swim away from Maxine screaming, 'Shark! Shark!' You guys are so silly!"

Gio laughed, which got water up her nose and made us all laugh even harder. Gio pinched her nose and said in a nasal voice, "You don't want her around us, anyway, do you?"

"Well, no," I admitted. "Because I've got something to tell you." Then I explained about helping with bathing the horses.

"Ooooh!" Gio's mouth formed a tiny o. "And I can come too?"

"Yes! Trish said I could bring somebody!"

"What about me?" Kaydence asked. "I'd like to help."

"I hope they'll let me bring a couple more people," I said. "I want to see if Ashton wants to come too."

"You're not going to ask Maxine to come along, are you?" Gio wrinkled her nose.

I shook my head. "No. She'll just take Misty away from me again," I said. "The whole point is so that I can have some time with Misty without her interfere—"

"SHARK!" Kaydence suddenly screamed again. I covered my ears.

"Shark! Shark! Look out!! SHARK!!!" Gio and Kaydence both started shouting again as they shot away from the approaching Maxine.

Here we go again, I thought, as I arched my arm to start swimming away. "Shark!" I yelled out (not as loudly as Kaydence and Gio). "Watch out! SHARK!!"

"Wait! Guys! Hey! Wait up!" Maxine called out behind us. "Kitty!"

I winced when I heard her use my nickname. And not turning around, I followed Gio and Kaydence as they streaked through pool again. Chopping at the water with our strokes and kicks, we passed by kids floating on inflatable rafts, having boogie board races, and pool noodle sword fights. We didn't stop until we were sure we had left Maxine lengths behind us again.

The three of us gathered at a corner of the pool before I sneaked a peek to see where Maxine was. I spotted her in the distance. Well, her head, anyway, floating just above the sparkling surface of the pool. She was staring at us. She looked confused. Or sad. Or angry. I wasn't sure. She was kind of far away and the sun was so bright I had to shield my eyes.

Then I started to feel a little funny in the pit of my stomach. "I don't know, guys," I said. "Isn't this kind of mean?"

"What's mean about it?" Kaydence said. "We're just playing!"

"Yeah," Gio said, churning the water with graceful arm movements. "This is just a game."

"I guess," I said as I reached for the nearby ladder and lifted my soggy body out of the pool with a heave. "I'm going to find Ashton and see if she wants to join us at the barn later."

"Okay," Gio said, adjusting the strap of her swimsuit so that it smoothed out. "But I mean it. Don't feel bad about the shark thing," she said.

"Yeah," Kaydence said. "We were just having fun. I mean, we're entitled to a little privacy, aren't we? She doesn't have to be with us all the time, does she?"

"No . . . she doesn't," I admitted. "You're right." But as I padded away from the two of them, leaving a trail of wet footprints on the tile, I hung my head. And while trying to shake off some pool water from my arms I noticed that I still had the funny feeling in my stomach, and I *couldn't* shake that off.

Just then I spotted Ashton, and I called her over to the side of the pool to ask if she wanted to help with the horses.

When I did, she repeated loudly, *"Wash* the *horses?"*

"Shhh! Not so loud!" I told her. "I don't know how many people are allowed to come with me. I need to check with Trish."

"Oh, okay! So, yeah, sure!"

"Okay, so just remember, don't tell anyone else—" I began, but Ashton swam away, leaving me to say to no one, "—I don't want to disappoint anyone if they can't come . . ."

I let out a deep breath. The truth was I didn't want Maxine finding out and insisting on coming along. Then I got that funny feeling in my stomach again. Like . . . guilt or something. *But why?* I wondered. Then the thought entered my head. *You're shutting Maxine out.* I shook my head. *That can't be right. I mean, I can't ask Maxine to come along. She would probably ruin everything. She'd hog Misty and all the attention from the counselors. Not to mention she would lie the whole time!* I shuddered at the scenario I pictured in my mind. *It would end up not being any fun at all. No, it's best not to mention it to her,* I told myself firmly. Then I straightened my shoulders. *Besides, I'm not even sure we'll be allowed to help with the horses. I still haven't asked for Sunny's permission!*

I quickly scanned the pool area and found her standing by the side of the pool, timing races between Heaven and Harmony. "That was a close one!" she shouted at the twins. "Heaven won by a second!"

"I'm Harmony!"

"Oh, sorry, Harmony! Got you two confused—" She turned to me because I had tapped her on the elbow. "Oh, hi, hun. What can I do for you?"

I told her about Trish's invitation to help with the horses. "Can I go? Maybe with some of the other girls?"

"Since it'll be your free time, that sounds fine. Just let me know who's going later, okay?"

"It'll be me and Gio for sure," I said. "Maybe a couple of other girls if it's all right with Trish."

"Yeah. I guess it depends on how many of you she can supervise at once," Sunny said. "Don't bring the whole cabin. You don't want to overwhelm her—or the horses. Maybe some of you can help today, some tomorrow, and others the next day."

I widened my eyes. That sounded like a great idea! I could hardly wait to suggest it to Trish. That way everyone in our cabin could have a turn. Including Maxine! Relief flowed through my body like a wave.

Then I got splashed—by what felt like a wave of water! I stood frozen in shock for a moment, soaked through and dripping. Then I slowly peered through the braids that were plastered against my face to see who had attacked me.

Maxine was standing just a few steps away from me, near the edge of the pool. She was holding an empty plastic bucket and laughing her head off. "Shark attack!" she said through her laughter.

I twisted my mouth up in a defeated smile. "You got me."

"Yup!" Then she turned away from me to look across the glistening surface of the water to spot two figures climbing out of the pool some distance away. Gio and Kaydence! A sneaky smile spread across her face. "And now to get my next victims . . ." And after bending down and scooping up a heavy bucketful of pool water, she began running in their direction.

I wondered if I should shout a warning to them when I heard someone call out, "Hey! Amber!"

It was Tangie, waving at me from the pool. "Want to race? Sunny will time us!"

"I—" Then I heard the SPLASH! And the shrieks from Gio and Kaydence. Too late to warn them, I grinned at Tangie and shrugged. "Okay!" And when Sunny nodded, I held my nose and dropped myself back into the pool.

Chapter 8

We had art next. I love art, and always took an opportunity to paint or draw something. What made art class even more fun, though, was that we got to do it outside and dry off in the hot sun at the same time.

Our art teacher, Counselor Sam, stood waiting for us just outside a playing field in a patch of ground set up with two picnic tables. A large cardboard box sat at his feet. He pointed to it and at the T-shirts in all sizes and colors that filled it. "Pick one out! You're going to get to play 'designer' today. On this table here," he pointed to his right, "we have rubber stamps with every letter of the alphabet and all kinds of fun designs. On this next table we have fabric paints in all colors for you to choose from. You can dip one of these tiny sponges in the paint and dab it on the stamp like this," he said, showing us quickly, "and then you can stamp your shirt up. Or, if you prefer, you can use a paintbrush or one of these fabric markers to write or draw with your own hand."

As he spoke, it was funny, because when he pointed to the cardboard box, we all went, "Ooooh!" and ran over to it to start looking through it. But when he said "stamps," we dropped the shirts back in the box and all rushed over to the table to look at what was there. Finally, when he mentioned paint and markers we ran over to *that* table to look at those.

Counselor Sam laughed, holding up his hands in protest. "Okay, everyone, calm down. You will all get a turn and be able to finish your shirt design before class is over. That is, if nobody hogs all the stamps or paints. You all have to share and cooperate with one another, okay?"

Ashton raised her hand. "Can we draw anything on the shirt or is it supposed to be something in particular?"

"Oh! I almost forgot to tell you! You're going to be designing T-shirts for your cabin team!" Sunny said. "Before you begin, you'll have to think up a name for your group."

"That's easy!" Gio said, and she began pumping her fist in the air and chanting, "Co-ries! Co-ries! Co-ries!"

Soon we were all chanting it. "Co-ries! Co-ries!"

"Okay, it sounds like you have a name!" Sunny chuckled. "But is that it? I mean, do you all want to call yourself, 'The Cories' or 'The Cori-somethings'? Or the something-Cories? Or . . . something?"

Kaydence tapped her mouth with her pointer finger as she thought it over. "'The Kind Cories'? 'The Creative Cories'?"

"'The Cori Chorus?' 'The Cori Choir?'" Heaven suggested.

"How about . . . *The Cori Corps*!" Maxine practically exploded with her idea.

"'The Cori-Core'?" Tangie sneered. "Like apple cores?"

"No, not like C-O-R-E, like C-O-R-P-S," Maxine spelled out.

It was Kaydence's turn to make a face. "Ew! *Corpse*? As in a dead body? No way!"

Maxine stamped her foot. "No! Not like a dead body!"

Sunny broke in, "'Corps' is *pronounced* 'core' but spelled like 'corpse' without the 'e' at the end," she explained. "But it does mean body. Just not a dead one. More like a 'body of people'

65

joined together to act as a team. You know, like how the body of Christ is the church. It's a word you will find used in the military. Like 'squad'!"

"A squad!" Everyone liked the idea after hearing that. "Okay, then let's just be The Cori Squad!"

"Great!" Counselor Sam pointed to the T-shirts in the box. "The only rule for the design of the shirt is that you're all supposed to make sure your team name is on it. You can paint it, write it, or stamp it—your choice. You might want to choose shirts in the same color, though, if you want to make them look more uniform. But you don't have to."

We all gathered around the huge box of T-shirts. There were so many beautiful colors to choose from, I didn't think we'd all be able to settle on just one. There was bright blue, sunflower yellow, soft lavender, spring green . . . but when I saw an orangey-pink color peeping through near the bottom of the pile, I knew it would be perfect. I reached in for it . . .

Snatch!

Suddenly it was in Maxine's hand, not mine. For a moment I thought she had just been trying to help me get it, so I smiled and held out my hand for her to hand it over. But instead she hugged the shirt to herself and announced, "I'm taking this one!"

"But . . ." I started to protest, but trailed off. I didn't want the counselors to think I was some kind of baby. Plus, I didn't think anyone had seen what she did. I bent down and dug deeper inside the box to see if I could find another shirt in that color. I had wanted to choose it because it was *coral* pink. The perfect color for "cories." So I was so glad when I found a bunch more together near the bottom.

I pulled them up and offered them to the others. "Anyone else want to have a coral colored shirt? Get it? Coral for Cories?"

"Oh, yeah!"

"Cool!"

"Okay, let's do that!"

"Copycats," Maxine muttered under her breath.

I ignored her and found a place at one of the picnic tables, hoping she'd stay far away from me. Unfortunately, she didn't. She stood facing me on the opposite side of the table.

Before we all started, Counselor Sam showed us all how to lay our T-shirts flat and to slip wax paper inside them so that the paint wouldn't bleed from the front to the back (or stick both sides together like glue).

Finally it was time to begin. I decided to use stamps to spell out the words "The Cori Squad" instead of writing the words out by hand. I found a nice, deep blue paint that I thought would look good against the coral, and I squeezed out a small glop onto a piece of aluminum foil. Next, I put down the tube of paint and began dabbing the paint on a stamp of the letter "C" when I noticed Maxine pick up the blue tube of paint and begin squeezing a blob onto *her* small sheet of aluminum foil.

I pressed the "C" onto the shirt and then rinsed and wiped the block for someone else to use. I found the stamp for the letter "O" next and picked it up at the same time I saw Maxine pick up the letter "C" stamp and begin to cover it in the same shade of blue that I had.

I stopped what I was doing to watch her as she pressed the "C" down in the same area on her T-shirt as I had on mine.

"Are . . . are you just going to do everything the same way I do it?" I asked, trying not to sound as annoyed as I felt.

"No," Maxine said. "It's not my fault you grabbed the stamps first. I was going to use them like this, anyway."

I didn't believe her. But I just said "Huh," in a doubtful tone.

As we continued to work, it became more and more annoying for me to see Maxine imitating my every move right after me and right before my eyes. When we were halfway through, I gritted my teeth. "You really should just make your own design," I told her.

"This *is* my own design!" she insisted.

At this, Heaven and Harmony both stopped what they were doing with their own shirts to look over at what was going on with us. (Maxine and I were at the end of the table. Harmony was next to me, and Heaven next to Maxine.) Even though they were identical twins, their designs were not identical. Heaven was making a tiny repeated pattern with a stamp of a koala bear. Harmony was using a brush and painting big flowers on her shirt by hand. When they realized what Maxine was doing, they exchanged glances with each other, said nothing, and went back to their designing.

I sighed deeply and went looking through the stamps. When I found a cute one of a horse, I decided to stamp it all around the collar so it looked like a necklace. The moment I put it down, though, of course, Maxine picked it up and did the same exact thing to her shirt. The only difference was that she messed up on one of the horses a little. It faded out a bit at the legs, so she tried pressing the stamp over the same spot, and ended up making the horse print a kind of double image—at least it sort of looked like it had eight legs.

"Oh, no!" she moaned.

I actually felt glad when that happened, but not because she

69

had messed up. (I would have been upset if that had happened to my shirt, and I felt bad seeing it happen to someone else's.) I was only glad because there was now a way to be able to tell our shirts apart!

But she began flapping her hands and yelling out, "Help me! Help me!" Counselor Sam was at her side in a flash to look over the damage.

"You can use a Q-tip to clean that up with some water," he told her in a soothing voice. "Do it now, though, before it dries. These are drying pretty fast under this sun."

"I can't!" Maxine whined. "I don't know how!"

Counselor Sam grabbed a cotton swab and dipped it in a small plastic bowl of water. "Like this. See?" He began to carefully wipe away the doubled image of the horse.

Great! I thought to myself. *So much for being able to tell them apart!*

When he was done, it *did* look better, but I noticed there was still a slightly blurry look to the image. Maxine noticed, too, and she groaned. "It's ruined!"

"No, it isn't! Not in the least! I mean, it's not perfect, but no one's shirt is perfect," Sam said. "I mean it, Maxine, take a look around you. I love the way they are all turning out. I think they look great! And it's their little imperfections that make them look more interesting. If they were all perfect and identical then they may as well have been made in a factory by machines." He patted her on the shoulder. "You're not a machine, Maxine. You're God's creation. Enjoy being creative like the Father." And he walked over to the next table.

Maxine crossed her arms and stared down at her shirt. She did not look convinced.

As I wondered what to do with my shirt next, Gio came over to my side. She opened her mouth to speak when she looked from my shirt to Maxine's and back again to mine. Then back to Maxine's. Then back at mine . . .

She crossed her arms. "Seriously?"

"Hi, Gio," I said, not wanting her to say anything and start an argument. "How's your shirt coming along?"

"Oh, great! I was just thinking that we should have a slogan for our cabin team. Then we can write them on our shirts. What do you think?"

"Yeah!" Tangie shouted from the next table.

"That's a great idea!" Ashton, who was next to her, agreed.

"I've got it!" Kaydence said. "Since we're from the *First* Letter to the Corinthians, how about, 'We're number one!'" She cackled at her own joke.

"Yeah!" Everybody jumped up and down.

"Um," Sunny broke in. "Considering that Scripture passage from chapter thirteen is all about how love is kind, and patient, and *doesn't boast*, is that really the most appropriate slogan?"

Kaydence laughed. "It's not boasting! It's telling the truth. You know, it is the *first* letter."

"Yeah, but don't forget what Jesus said," Ashton spoke up, "the last shall be first and the first shall be last. If we put that on our shirts, we'll probably end up coming in last in all our competitions."

This made us all laugh some more.

"Good point. So, yeah, maybe not that for a slogan, then," Kaydence admitted. "Can you read the Scripture to us again?" she asked Sunny.

"Sure." Sunny took out her phone and looked it up. "'Love

is patient, love is kind. It does not envy, it does not boast, it is not proud. It does not dishonor others, it is not self-seeking, it is not easily angered, it keeps no record of wrongs. Love does not delight in evil but rejoices with the truth. It always protects, always trusts, always hopes, always perseveres. Love never fails. But—"

She didn't need to continue, because everyone shouted out at the same time, "Love never fails!" It was short, powerful, and perfect.

"Okay! I guess you found your slogan, then," Sunny said, putting her phone away.

I flipped my T-shirt over to write the slogan on the back. I decided to write the words near the bottom so that when I wore it with my hair down my braids wouldn't cover it. And since the words were God's words, I decided that the best color to use would be gold. Finding a small jar of gold paint, I grabbed a paintbrush and tried to make the letters look as neat and as fancy as I could, but it wasn't easy. It made me wish Lena was at camp with us so that I could ask her to do if for me. She knew how to make pretty, decorative letters with markers. She did it all the time at home on the chalkboard wall in our playroom or in her journal.

When I finished the lettering I put down the brush and decided I needed to let the words dry before trying to do anything more on the shirt. But when I saw Maxine take the brush, dip it in the gold paint, and start writing our slogan on the back of *her* T-shirt, I lost my patience and walked away. *Now's a good time to see what the others are doing*, I decided.

I looked at Ashton's first. She had found a cute soccer ball stamp and was using it to decorate the sleeves of her T-shirt. Nobody else had thought to decorate their sleeves, so I thought that was pretty cool. Kaydence had written the words "CORI SQUAD in super-giant letters on the front on her shirt and had painted three hearts around them in a kind of glittery paint. The heart on top of the word "Cori" said "Love." The heart in between the words "Cori" and "Squad" said "Never" and the heart underneath "Squad" said "Fails."

Gio had painted the outline of a horse on her shirt, with just the mane and tail painted in. The words "The Cori Squad" were printed above it. "Love Never Fails" was written in script underneath it.

"These are really cool!" I said. What I especially liked was how different they all were. *I bet if Maxine had thought up a design all by herself it would have been cool too.* I thought when I returned to the table and watched her put the finishing flourish on the "s" in "Fails." *Too bad we'll never know.*

Soon it was time to clean up.

"Leave the shirts where they are so that they can finish drying," Sam said. "Just tidy up the rest."

We quickly cleared off the tables and set our shirts aside before assembling into a line to go to our next activity.

"What's coming up now? Do you know?" Ashton asked me.

I wiggled my eyebrows. "Pop Psalms."

"*Pop songs?*"

"No! Pop *psalms.* You know, like from the Bible," Gio explained. "P-S-A-L—wait a minute. Why aren't we moving?"

Yeah, why was that? I wondered. Then I noticed Sunny cup her mouth with her hands.

"Maxine, just leave your shirt to dry," she called out. "No one's going to take it. We'll bring them to our cabin later! Let's go."

Maxine, who for some reason was hovering over her shirt, nodded. Then, after smoothing it down a little, she finally joined the line.

"What were you doing?" I heard Heaven ask her.

"Just checking something," Maxine said.

"Great, now that we're all here we can go sing!" Sunny thrust her arm in front of her like a battering ram and began to run. "Charge!"

Whooping and laughing we all began running after her.

Panting as she ran, Gio grinned at me. "I know you must be looking forward to *this* class, Amber!"

"I sure am!" I said. I began singing, "I know it's my time . . . my time to step up . . !"

Chapter 9

At first I was half-skipping, half-jogging my way to the D.A.V.I.D. cabin, which was the big wooden building where we were supposed to gather for music classes. But the closer we got to the cabin the slower I got. I found my mind going back to Maxine.

What had she been doing? I asked myself. Then, narrowing my eyes, I snuck a sidelong glance at Maxine. We had put all the shirts on one table to dry side-by-side and put all the art supplies on the other table. *Did she finally put something on her shirt that was different than mine so that we could tell them apart?* Just as I looked at her, Maxine turned around to look back at the shirts herself. Suddenly my heart started pounding faster. *Or did she swap them?*

At that moment we all reached the front steps of the cabin and began walking up and inside, where I saw that a raised platform was set up on one side of the room, just like in the cafeteria. Only this stage had a lot of stuff on it, like folding chairs, music stands, and instruments (most of them still inside their cases). On the wall behind it was a large, flat TV screen, and lining some of the walls was a variety of sound equipment on carts or tables. Opposite all of this was a bunch of chairs facing the platform, where all of us campers were supposed to sit. As I chose a seat between Ashton and Gio, kids from other cabins started coming in, too, and soon the room was filled up.

"This will be fun, won't it?" Gio whispered in my left ear.

"Mm-hmm," I agreed between my firmly pressed lips. But my mind was not on the class I was about to have. I kept thinking about Maxine. One moment I was convincing myself that she wouldn't dare swap our shirts. The next minute I was sure she'd done exactly that. Our shirts were basically identical. She'd tried to copy it line for line, color for color, stamp for stamp. The only difference, of course, was that hers had that blurred horse stamping that had upset her. My *shirt didn't have a blurry horse . . .*

But my worries were interrupted when two counselors, Robert and Sharon, introduced themselves and explained that the class was called "Pop Psalms" because they had taken the music of popular songs from the radio and exchanged the song lyrics with Scripture verses from the psalms.

"The psalms were originally written as songs, although without music and on the printed page they seem more like poems," Robert said. He was tall and thin, and although he was a young man, he was already losing his hair in the front. He continued, "We know King David wrote many of them and that he was a skilled musician and songwriter. Basically, he was all about praise music."

Sharon, who had brown skin and a mane of long, super-curly golden hair, added, "He also danced in celebration of God's glory. That's why we named the cabin for the arts after him. The first letters of the words dance, art, vocal music, instrumental music, and drama spell out the name 'David.'"

Robert gestured at the TV screen behind him and it suddenly turned on. The words of a psalm filled the screen. "We thought this would be a fun way to teach you some music too! You know, with tunes you already know and Scriptures you already know." He picked up a microphone that had been lying on a chair and turned that on. "And who doesn't love karaoke?"

Ashton and Gio both turned their heads toward me and whispered at the same time, "Holy karaoke!"

My shoulders shook with silent laughter.

"Actually, let's all start with Psalm 8," Sharon said. "When I start up the music most of you will recognize the tune, only you'll be singing the words you see on the screen instead."

Once we began, the campers around me all seemed to pick up the tune very quickly. So when Sharon invited them to join in, the room was quickly filled with confident singing. But since I didn't listen to pop music much at all (unless it was Christian pop) I had to actually learn the tune while everyone was singing along. I felt a little behind everyone else. Like I was running to catch up. And even though Ashton was having the same problem, it didn't seem to bother her as much as it did me. Probably because I liked singing more than she did. Plus, she wasn't as distracted by worries as I was.

When we got to the next psalm and began to sing, I remembered how God's name is "I Am." Then I thought about the poem I had written, and how, when I had started writing it, Sunny had said something to Maxine about keeping her eyes on her own work. Then, how a short while afterwards, Maxine had even hidden her poem under the table. *Why had she done that?* I wondered. *Had she copied my poem the same way she had my shirt?*

I kept trying to talk myself out of imagining that Maxine

would swap my shirt with hers. But then I remembered other things, like how she'd taken my kitty coat right out of my trunk without asking. How she'd snatched the conditioner straight out of my hands. How she'd even taken Misty away from me by throwing a fit . . .

Then we sang again about praising God, and once more I remembered my poem. Only this time I remembered how I had pointed out that the "Am" in "Amber" was a part of God's name. At this memory I smacked myself on the forehead. *Why hadn't I just written my name on the shirt somewhere?* I thought frustratedly. Then I panicked. *What if that's what Maxine had done? What if she'd written* her *name on* my *shirt instead?*

Ashton flashed me a look of concern. "What's the matter?" she asked.

"You okay?" Gio asked from my other side.

"Yeah, I'm fine, I . . . I . . . " *I have to go back to that picnic table, that's what,* I told myself. *I need to know!* "I have to, uh, do something," I said.

Ashton gave me a look. "*Now?*"

"I'll explain later," I whispered to her.

I jumped out of my chair and excused myself. But instead of heading for the bathroom (like I had to pretend in order to leave), I sprinted toward the art tables. When I got there (a little breathless), Counselor Sam was picking up the shirts from the table. Both my shirt and Maxine's were already gone. I guessed they were in the small stack over his arm.

"Wait!" I held up a hand and used the other to press down on a cramp in my side as I caught my breath.

"Don't worry, they're dry," Counselor Sam said. He ran his hand over the horse on Gio's shirt. "See?"

I nodded. "Yes. I mean, no." I shook my head and swallowed. "I mean . . . I forgot to put my name on my shirt!"

"That's not a problem," Sam said. "You know which one's yours, don't you?"

I reached for the small stack in his arms. "I do. But Maxine made hers . . . look a lot like mine," I said, trying to be nice about it. "I don't want them to get mixed up."

"Oh, well, it should be right here." He quickly rummaged through them. "Here! This is it, isn't?"

"It *looks* like mine," I said hesitatingly. "Uhhh . . ." I looked it over carefully. "No. This one's Maxine's actually." I pointed to the smeary horse. "See?"

Sam frowned at it. "Oh, yeah, you're right. I tried my best to fix that."

"So, um, can I please put my name on *mine* so that Maxine and I don't get them confused?"

"Sure." Sam peeled my T-shirt from the pile in his arms. "That must mean that this one is yours. Oh, no, wait. This one says 'Max' on it,"

"*What?*"

He leaned down to show me. There, on the front of my shirt near the bottom, just above the hem, were three capital letters in tiny handwriting: MAX.

"But that's wrong!" I blurted. "This is my shirt! See?" I pointed to the row of horses at the collar. They were all neat and evenly printed.

"Oh. Yeah. Well, I guess it was an honest mistake. You know you guys made them look exactly the same."

"No, we didn't . . ." I said under my breath. Out loud, I said, "What am I going to do? This is written with fabric marker. It won't wash off!"

"Why don't you just keep hers and you let her have yours? They're like clones of each other, anyway," Sam said with a smile.

Why didn't he understand? "No! I want *my* shirt! The one I worked on!" I felt tears starting to rise up in my eyes. I blinked them back down.

"Okay, okay," Sam seemed alarmed to see that I was getting upset. "Let's see, what are your options? Well, you can scribble it out, but that probably won't look so good. You can try stamping over it with something. Or we can cut it out. You know, cut an inch off the bottom of the T-shirt."

I didn't like any of the choices, but they seemed to be the only choices I had. "Can we . . . can we try a stamp?" I asked in a sad voice.

"Sure!" Sam opened a tin full of them. "Let's pick one that can cover those letters up. And if we can't, we can always just cut it off."

I sighed and began looking through the selection of designs. There were lots of pretty ones, but most of them wouldn't look right just stamped onto the bottom of my shirt for what would look like no good reason. Then I saw it. The perfect stamp. "This one!"

"The sleeping cat? Okay." Sam took it out and held it over Max's name to see if it would cover it over. "This might work. We'll use gold paint."

After using a brush to carefully cover the stamp, he pressed it over Max's name. When he took it off, the image on the shirt looked neat and even, but I could still see some of the letters showing through.

"This is where my art degree comes in," Sam said. "I can cover that up with some more paint and make it look like the fur on the cat's body. That is, if that's okay with you."

I nodded. "Yes! Yes! Please!"

The tip on his brush was very fine, and the delicate lines he painted with his very steady hand matched the look of the stamp very well.

"Now, why don't you sign your name next to it so that we don't have this mix-up again?"

I nodded, and taking the brush, wrote "Amber" as neatly as I could.

Sam wrote "Max" at the bottom of Max's shirt. "There! Now it's all taken care of. You'd better get back to your voice class. I'll clean up while it dries."

"Thank you *so* much!" I said, feeling light with relief.

"No problem," Sam said with a wave.

After saying goodbye to him, I headed back to the D.A.V.I.D. cabin at a jog instead of a flat-out run like before, deciding, this time I'll trot back instead of galloping!

When I got back to the music room it was practically vibrating with all the singing voices. They washed over me in a comforting wave of sound. *I can relax now*, I thought as I made my way back to my chair. When I got back to my seat, Ashton and Gio looked at me with curiosity in their eyes, but I just smiled and nodded to let them know I'd tell them later. I sat back and closed my eyes for a moment. *Thank you for letting me know that Maxine had put her name on the wrong shirt,* I told God, *so that I could fix it.* But when I opened my eyes I was still left with one unanswered question. *Had Maxine done that by accident or on purpose?*

Figure it out, later, Amber, I told myself. *Now it's time for praise.* And after taking a deep breath, I began to sing.

Chapter 10

I explained everything to Ashton and Gio as we headed back to our cabin to freshen up before lunch.

"Oooh! The nerve!" Ashton balled her hands up in fists. "Why can't she leave your stuff alone?"

"You should tell on her," Gio said. "She needs to get in trouble for that sort of thing so she won't do it again!"

"Tell on her?" I repeated. "For what? I'm not even sure she did it on purpose."

"Of course she did it on purpose," Gio said.

Ashton tilted her head. "I think she did it on purpose, too, but you can't really prove it. So, you're right, it's best not to say anything."

"If she pulled something like that on me," Gio said, "I'd tell her off. She needs to keep her hands to herself *and* her stuff!"

Just then, Maxine ran past us to get to the cabin first. When I stepped inside with Ashton and Gio, Maxine was saying, "Oh, look! Our T-shirts are here!" She reached out for the stack of shirts that was lying on top of one of the trunks and pawed through it. Taking one out, she looked at it carefully. "Here's mine!" she said, spotting her name on the bottom. She began handing me mine when the golden cat caught her eye. "What's that?"

"It's a kitty," I said. "Get it?"

"Yeah, but, when did you do that?"

I didn't want to answer her. "When did you put *your* name on *your* T-shirt?"

Maxine looked down at her name and frowned. She looked very confused. Then she shrugged to herself and turned to me with a smile. "You know, our shirts look so much alike we can swap them! Want to?"

"Um, no," I said, feeling my body stiffen at the idea. "My shirt has my name on it and your shirt has yours."

"But that'll make it even more fun!"

"I want to wear the shirt *I* made," I said. "In fact, I'm going to change into it right now so that I can wear it—um, this afternoon." I'd almost said, "at the barn."

Maxine immediately brightened. "I'm going to wear mine too!" she said cheerfully.

"Of course you are," Gio said. I didn't see her roll her eyes, but I could tell by the tone of her voice that she had.

Ashton, who passed me in the long bathroom on the way to her room, whispered in my ear, "She's not just a copycat, she's a copy*kitty*."

I flashed her a tired smirk.

We were finally all headed to the cafeteria when I saw Counselor Trish in the distance. I knew I had to ask her if bringing three other girls with me would be okay, but I didn't want Maxine to see me—or worse, follow me. So I waited until a crowd of us were all walking through the doors to back out without being seen and ran over to Trish.

She was talking to Counselor Iris, but stopped when she saw me and bent down a little. "Yes, Amber?"

"I'm still helping with the horse bathing this afternoon, right?" I asked, panting a little. "And I can bring a friend?"

"Yeah! It'll be fun!"

"Oh, I know, it's just that . . . well, another friend heard about it, and my twin sister too. Um, can I bring some others?"

Iris and Trish exchanged glances. Trish wrinkled her forehead with worry. "Are we talking about your whole cabin, here? Because then we're talking about having a class, basically. I won't be able to do that . . ."

"No, just two more. Uh, four of us altogether."

Iris nudged Trish and nodded. "I'll take the other two. They can help me muck and wash and stuff."

Trish sighed with relief. "Okay, so your sis and the other girl will work with Iris," she said. "Come right after lunch!"

"Thanks!" I said, and I turned to go. But then I turned back. "One more thing," I said, with a nervous giggle. "The other girls in our cabin might be upset about not being able to come with us. Is it . . . can they . . . would you let them help too? Like, tomorrow? Or the next day?"

"That's a nice idea. Okay, sure, let's say tomorrow afternoon at the same time as today. You can let them know now, though, so they won't get jealous," Iris said.

I jumped in the air. "Thank you! See you later! Or, soon! Or . . . in a bit!" I said, laughing and waving as I ran back to the cafeteria. I didn't want Maxine to see me walking in with the two of them.

I found my table mates standing in line to get their lunches. I was glad to be a bit behind them so that I could get some more apple slices—and even some carrots this time—without Maxine asking me questions.

Ashton, Kaydence, and Gio slid me questioning looks and I gave them all a "thumbs up" so that they'd know that we were good to go after lunch.

As we sat down to eat, I noticed that there were instruments and equipment set up on the stage: a drum set, some microphones in stands, even a keyboard. As I took a bite out of my turkey sandwich, Ms. Cameron went up to the stage and tapped the microphone in the middle.

"Ladies and gentlemen," she said. "May I have your attention, please? Let me introduce to you, for your lunchtime listening pleasure, the famous . . ." she stretched out her hand, "DoveSword!"

Five counselors came up onto the stage and waved as we hooted, hollered, and clapped our welcome.

Counselor Sharon, one of the choral teachers from the class we'd just had, took center stage and adjusted the microphone to her height. This made me smile because she was on the smaller side, like me. "Yes, that's right, we're your counselors by day, but at night—and, er, at lunchtime—we become DoveSword! Named after the Holy Spirit, twice. Because, as you all know, in the Bible doves represent the Holy Spirit. But also, in Paul's letter to the Ephesians, the 'sword of the Spirit' is one of the pieces of the armor of God. Doves are also used to symbolize peace, and God is peace. But Jesus is also our sword, our best weapon in spiritual battles. So whether we are in times of peace or in times of trouble what's most important is that we trust and praise Him, right, everyone?"

"Right!" All around the room heads were nodding and fists were pumping in the air.

Sharon introduced her band members: Robert was there, of course, on the lead guitar. Gus, from the barn, was on bass. Iris, also from the barn, was behind the keyboard, and Sam, the T-shirt guy, was in the back on the drums. It was then that I noticed they were all wearing matching red T-shirts with a dove and a sword painted on them. I wondered if Sam had made them all or if they had each made their own, like we did.

"This is a song that Iris wrote, actually," Sharon said, "called, 'Dig It Up.' It's based on a parable found in Matthew 25:14–30, and how the best way to say 'thank you' to God for any gift he gives you is to use it!" She pointed at Sam and he began to pound out a beat. Then Sharon began to sing,

The master's on the road,
We've seen him on the way.
Oh, we knew he'd be here soon,
But didn't know it'd be today!
What have I got to give him,
Is there something I can present?
It must be from the heart,
Maybe I can use my talent.
But it's buried in dirt.
It's time to dig it up.
I hope I'm not too late
To dig it up, dig it up, dig it up, dig it up . . .

The music had us all bopping in our seats. Especially the drums, since they marked a beat after every "up."

"Isn't that cool that our counselors have a band?" Kaydence said.

"*We* should make a band!" Gio said. "We should *be* a band! A Cori Squad band!"

"Yeah!" the other girls at the table all agreed.

"And *you* can be the lead singer," Gio told me. "Since you're the singer in this group."

"And *I'll* be the drummer!" Maxine yelled out.

I turned to her in surprise. "Oh! Do you know how to play?"

"No," Maxine shrugged. "But it can't be that hard."

Kaydence cupped her chin with her hand. "Oh, sure. Uh-huh. Easy. All you need is coordination. And to keep a beat. But since you can't post a trot, let alone even ride a horse—"

"I can *too* ride a horse!" Maxine fumed. "What do you think I was doing today?"

"Bouncing all over the place, that's what," Kaydence shot back.

I held out my hands trying to get them to settle down. "Um, actually, do *any* of you guys know how to play *any* instruments?"

"Uh . . ." Everyone looked at each other. Little by little embarrassed smiles started to break across everyone's face until we were all giggling. "No . . ." everyone admitted.

"Except you, Amber. You know some ukulele and some piano," Ashton said.

"Yeah." I took a sip of my orange juice. "But did you hear what Sharon said? Iris *wrote* that song. I don't know how to write songs!"

"But you can write poems," Gio reminded me. "And isn't that kind of the same thing?"

I thought about it for a moment. "Kind of, I guess."

"Anyway," Maxine said in a voice that clearly meant, "let's change the subject." "Are we all going to have that Winter Sisters singalong during free time?"

I almost choked on my bite of turkey sandwich. I'd completely forgotten about it. I shot a panicked look at Ashton.

"Let's do that tonight, after dinner," Ashton announced. "It's more of a slumber party thing, don't you think?"

Everyone seemed to like that idea.

"Then what shall we do after lunch?" Maxine asked, without missing a beat. "What do you want to do?" she asked me.

At that moment DoveSword finished performing and the applause filled the cafeteria. I put down my sandwich to join in the clapping and hoped that Maxine would forget she was waiting for an answer to her question. And she did, for about a minute, but then Counselor Iris made her way to the table.

"Hi, girls! What did you think?"

We practically jumped out of our seats to tell her how good she'd been.

"Your band rocks!" Kaydence said.

"Thank you!" Iris said. Her cheeks reddened, reminding me of two apples. "But all the glory goes to God! I just came by to see if any of you are ready." She turned to me. "Which two will be coming with me?"

Chapter 11

Um . . ." I sank in my chair as all the eyes at the table focused on me. Then, after clearing my throat (which suddenly felt dry and scratchy) I managed to croak, "Kaydence and Ashton."

"Great!" Iris said brightly as Kaydence and Ashton sat up straighter in their chairs. "Whenever you guys are ready, you can come with me to the barn."

Grinning widely, Kaydence and Ashton started clearing off their trays. Also smiling, Gio began to get ready too. But Heaven, Harmony, Tangie, and Maxine looked confused. Maxine was blinking so fast I thought for a minute that she had something in her eye. "Huh?" she said.

Iris's eyebrows shot up her forehead. "Didn't Amber tell y'all? Oh, I guess I must have ruined your surprise. Four of you are going to help out at the barn after lunch today. And the other four will help on Wednesday. That is, if you want."

Gio jumped in to make sure it was clear. "Amber and I are helping today too. We're going to give the horses a bath."

"So, what about you other girls? You want to help out on Wednesday?"

Heaven and Harmony clapped and nodded enthusiastically.

Tangie still looked a little confused, but agreed as well.

Maxine slapped down hard on the tabletop. "No!"

The rest of us at the table all sighed at the same time.

"I want to help *today*!" Max whined. "Why can't I go today with Amber's group?"

"Because we're only taking four at a time," Iris said firmly. "But don't worry, you'll get your chance."

Maxine wriggled in her seat. "Switch with me, Ashton," she pouted. "You're from the other bedroom. All *your* bunkmates are going on Wednesday. You should go with them. I should be going with mine."

"Amber and Gio and Kaydence *were* my bunkmates until you decided not to sleep in that room. Remember? I already gave up my spot for you once." Amber shook her head. "Not this time."

Kaydence and Gio each crossed their arms.

"I'm not switching," Gio said.

"Me neither," Kaydence claimed.

Maxine sunk down in her seat. "This isn't fair!"

Sunny, who had been chatting with other counselors at another table, came over when she heard all the raised voices. "Can I help?"

"Some of the . . ." Iris caught sight of my shirt, ". . . the Cori Squad are coming to help with the horses during break time. But we can only take four at a time. The other four can help tomorrow. This one's upset because she wanted to help today and doesn't want to have to wait."

"Come on, Maxine. Helping with the horses during break time is a treat, not a right. You should just be grateful and look forward to tomorrow. Good things come to those who wait, after all," said Sunny.

"Fine!" Maxine stood up and raised her nose in the air. "Maybe we'll do our own singalong while you're all gone, right girls?"

Heaven and Harmony stayed silent, not agreeing or disagreeing.

Tangie looked like she wanted to dive under the table.

Maxine answered herself, "Well, we will! And we won't wait for *you* all to do it!" And even though she said "all" she pointed only at me. Then she flounced away from the table.

"Her feelings were hurt," Sunny said sadly.

"Her feelings are *always* hurt," Gio griped.

"Some people are more sensitive than others," Sunny said. "That's just how it is. Not everyone thinks or feels the same. We have to try to be more understanding of others."

Kaydence raised her arms in surrender. "Only if we don't think or feel the same way as other people do, how can we understand them?"

Sunny patted her on the shoulder. "That's where prayer comes in. We pray to the Holy Spirit for the gift of understanding. I'm going to go check on her. You girls finish up and have fun at the barn!"

Iris nudged Tangie. "So you're okay with tomorrow?"

"Yeah." Tangie got up, pushing back her chair. It scraped across the floor with a sound that would have been louder if the cafeteria wasn't so noisy. "I was kind of looking forward to the singalong this afternoon, too, though." She darted a quick look in my direction. "But I guess I can wait until tonight. Maybe I'll do my nails. Or, I know! I'll read one of my books!"

"You brought books?" Harmony stared at her open-mouthed.

"To *camp*?" Heaven added.

Tangie's face lit up. "Yeah. The Narnia series. Maybe I'll read out on the deck."

"Wait, the whole series?" I asked. "All seven books?"

"Yeah! I mean, they're not very big. And they're paperbacks. I just love them."

"But you've read them *before*?" Harmony pressed, making sure she understood.

"Sure. A few times."

"You read books more than once?"

"You *don't*?" Tangie asked both twins.

Iris laughed and waved at those of us going to the barn. "Come on, let's not keep the horses waiting."

After getting rid of our trash, Ashton, Gio, Kaydence, and I followed Iris back to the barn. Then we split up. Trish waved me and Gio over to her side while Ashton and Kaydence continued on with Iris to another section of the barn.

"Hi, girls!" Trish said. "As you can see, I've got Misty all ready for her beauty treatment." Misty was tied to a fence, eating out of a bag of hay as she waited patiently to be scrubbed down.

I patted Misty on her neck. "Oh, she doesn't need beauty treatments! She's gorgeous all on her own."

"That's true. I guess we're going to pamper her a bit, then. She's been so good to us, it's time we return the favor, don't you think?"

First Trish gave me and Gio some body brushes to sweep the dust and grime off Misty's coat. "And don't forget the tail. Bits of hay can get all tangled up in there."

"Got it," Gio said. She began combing out the tail with such effort and concentration that she ended up sticking her tongue out of the side of her mouth the whole time.

"Now we soak her down." Trish signaled at me to hand her the hose that lay curled up nearby. When I did, she told us, "Now we have to be careful. This hose has been out in the sun, so it's

93

kind of hot. Always let it run a little first before you use it so that the water cools down." When she was satisfied with the water's temperature, Trish handed the hose to me. "You do this side, Amber. Then when she's done, Gio, you'll do the other." And as I ran the hose over Misty in what I was sure was a refreshing shower, Trish stroked Misty's cheek. "Now doesn't that feel good after being out in the hot sun all day?"

Next we shampooed and conditioned Misty all over.

"This is kind of like washing my dad's car," Gio said as she rubbed in the shampoo. "Only better."

As I smeared the conditioner all over Misty's mane and tail, I smiled to myself. It reminded me of when I had conditioned my own hair earlier. Soon I was imagining Misty jumping off the diving board and swimming laps in the pool. It was such a silly picture in my head that by the time I passed the hose to Gio again, I was giggling.

When we were done, Misty seemed to hold her head up proudly as she pranced in place. It looked almost like she was dancing.

"I think she's happy to be clean," I said.

"It does feel good to get all cleaned up, doesn't it?" Trish placed her hands on her hips as she looked over the job we did. "She knows she looks good too."

Seeing how pleased Misty seemed to be made me feel warm inside. I placed a hand over my heart. "I like knowing that I helped to make her happy," I said.

"Yes, many animals serve man. And they serve their purpose under God when they do. But we have as much—or more—responsibility to serve those animals right back. It's our duty to take good care of them," Trish said. "They work hard for us. They also make life more fun for us. But we have to feed them and keep them healthy and clean in return."

"But it doesn't *feel* like work," Gio said. "Because we love them!"

"I'm glad you feel that way, Gio," Trish said with a sly grin. She handed us two pitchforks that had been leaning against the fence. "Because keeping them healthy and clean means mucking out their stalls and putting in new straw too."

"I spoke too soon," Gio said, pinching her nose with one hand and grabbing a pitchfork with the other.

As we freshened Misty's stall, I noticed movement over at the washing station. Trish was bringing Blessing over to be washed next.

"Ooh!" I said, wiping my forehead with my forearm. "Can we show Gio Blessing's secret?"

Trish nodded as she tied Blessing's lead rope to a nearby fencepost. "Of course. But first let's see how you two did." Once our work got her seal of approval, Trish led Misty back into her stall. "Isn't it wonderful?" she murmured to Misty. "Now both you and your room are nice and fresh!"

Then I got to show Gio the cross on Blessing's forehead. She gasped. "That is so cool! Oh! Can I ride Blessing Wednesday?"

"I thought you loved Jackson!" I reminded her.

"Oh! I do! And I want to ride Jackson too! I want to ride both of them!"

The truth was, I wanted to ride *both* Misty and Blessing myself. So I understood what Gio meant. "I almost forgot," I said, reaching into my pocket for the apples and carrots I had wrapped in the napkin. "Want to give some to Jackson?"

"Oh, can I?" Gio held out her hands so that I could pour out pieces of apples and carrots into them. Then, leaning over to catch Trish's eye, she repeated, "Can I?"

Trish pointed to where Jackson was. "Go ahead."

"Thanks!" Gio hurried over to give him his treats.

"You too," Trish said, letting me know I could give Blessing his treats.

As Blessing ate out of my hand, I got that same warm feeling that I had before when I'd seen how happy Misty was to be clean. *It's good to be kind to animals*, I thought to myself, *but it also* feels *good to be kind to animals.*

After giving Blessing a bath like Misty's, I started playing with a section of his long mane and made a tiny braid.

"Do you want us to do his hair?" Trish asked.

"What?" I asked. "Can we?"

"Why not?" Trish said. "Let me just get some braid bands. I'll be right back."

When she returned, she was holding a plastic jar filled with what looked like hundreds of tiny black hair bands. "Let's not make tiny braids, though. That will take more time than we have. Let's do a big diamond braid out of his whole mane. Wait till you see it. It's really pretty."

When she said it would be a braid of the whole mane, I thought it would be something like a French braid straight down his spine. But it wasn't at all.

"This looks more like macramé, than a braid," Trish said.

"Like we're weaving his mane into a shawl," I said.

Trish guided us into making a row of ponytails that hung down the right side of Blessing's neck. Then, we'd split the ponytails and tie half of one with half of the other one next to it,

making diamond-shaped spaces between them. When we were done, it looked very fancy.

"This looks way harder to make than it is!" I said, when we were done.

"Great job, girls! It's a masterpiece!" Trish said.

Throwing my arms around Blessing's neck, I gave him a gentle hug and whispered, "You're just beautiful!"

I told Ashton all about it when we headed back to our cabin.

"It sounds like you crocheted his mane!" Ashton laughed. "That reminds me, I told Rani I would make a granny square for her while I was here, so she could have a Camp Caracara square to add to her quilt."

Rani was a friend of ours who had moved to England. A month back, our other friend, Jasmyn, taught us all how to crochet "granny squares" which were small yarn squares you could attach together to make one bigger piece, like a shawl or a throw. We (even Ansley and Lena) were all making squares so that Jasmyn could put them together into one prayer shawl for Rani.

"Ooh, can you show me how to make a square?" Gio asked Ashton.

"Sure! Remind me later."

"You'd better not make a square while you're here, Amber," Gio told me.

"What? Why not?"

"Because! Then Maxine will want to make one just like it!"

"Oh," I laughed a little. "Yeah."

"You know," Gio said, stopping in the middle of an open field. "I don't know why you don't speak up and tell Maxine to stop being such a copycat. Why do you keep letting her get away with everything?"

My guts started to squirm inside my belly. "I don't know. She's not that bad. I'm just trying to be . . . you know, patient and kind."

"Meanwhile, she just keeps on being a pain. And it's only going to get worse if you don't say something soon," Gio said. "And you're not going to like it! You'll see . . . !"

I waved away what she said and continued on to the cabin, leading the rest of the way there. Once we were close, I broke into a jog. I wanted to make sure I got to freshen up before our Bible study class, which was coming up next. "Beat you there!" I teased the others.

"Oh, no, you don't!" Ashton said, passing me.

I shrieked in surprise and sped up. Soon we were in a neck-and-neck race to the cabin.

We hit the deck at the same time, and I caught a glimpse of Heaven and Harmony playing cards and Tangie reading a book. I stretched out to grab hold of the door first and yanked it open. "I win!"

Maxine, who was lying on her bed, jumped in surprise. "You guys almost scared me to death!" she said. Then she quickly shoved a notebook under her pillow.

"What's that?" I asked.

Maxine scratched the back of her head. "What?"

I pointed. "What you hid under your pillow."

"Nothing."

"It was a notebook," I said.

"Well, if you know it's a notebook," Maxine sneered, "then why did you ask me what it was?"

"It's just that—never mind!" I muttered. Ashton and I exchanged glances and she went to her room and Kaydence and Gio came running through the door. I went over to my trunk to get another shirt to wear because unfortunately my new Cori Squad T-shirt was already covered in dirt and dust and hay. When I opened my trunk, though, I found my poem sitting on top of all my clothes. *That wasn't there before*, I thought to myself. *Hadn't I put that in the side pocket?* Suddenly feeling Maxine's eyes on me, I looked up. Maxine looked away and began scribbling in her notebook.

She's acting weird, I thought. *Something's definitely up with her. And I'll bet Gio was right: when I find out what it is, I'm not going to like it!*

Chapter 12

Our Bible study class was taught by Sunny, who brought us down to the lake.

"I like to use this spot for praying," Sunny told us, "because there are lots of places to sit in the shade near the peaceful waters."

"It's kind of like Psalm 23," Ashton said. "He makes me lie down in green pastures, he leads me beside quiet waters, he refreshes my soul . . ."

"You know, I didn't even think of that," Sunny said. "But you're absolutely right. That's why it's so perfect!"

Then, after instructing us to all sit in a circle on the grass, Sunny showed us a blue baseball cap with the logo of a dove and a sword on it. "Inside this cap there are a number of folded up slips of paper. Written on each slip is a Scripture verse. You will all take turns picking one out of the cap. Then you will look it up in the Bible—there's a stack on that bench over there—and sit and pray over what you read. To do this, you guys will have to split up. Everyone needs to be by themselves to meditate. But you can't go so far away that I can't see you. No further than that tree, that table, and that garbage can, okay?" She pointed out the boundaries. "As you are all doing that, I will be taking turns sitting with each one of you to go over your verse and what it says to your heart."

As the hat made its way toward me, I felt myself growing excited. I hoped I would end up picking a really cool one that meant something special to me. Finally, when the hat was in front of me I closed my eyes, which was funny because all the slips of paper looked the same, and reached inside. I carefully pulled out a piece of paper, passed the hat on to the next camper, and unfolded the slip. It read:

Luke 6:27–31

Oh good, it's from one of the Gospels, I thought. That meant it would probably be something Jesus said.

"Go get a Bible and pick a place to sit," Sunny urged me.

Taking the Bible at the top of the stack on the bench, I looked around until I found a private-looking spot. It was perfect, really. With a big rock to lean on, a bush that half-hid me from view, and the shade of an overhead tree, it looked cozy. I settled down with a sigh and closed my eyes for a moment just to feel the sun on my legs and hear the lapping sounds of the nearby lake. It sounded so soft it was like someone had put lotion in the water.

If I was Gio I'd fall asleep right now, I thought with a smile. *But I'm not, so . . .* I opened my eyes and began to look up the verse. "Here it is," I said to myself out loud. Then I read under my breath: "But to you who are listening I say: Love your enemies, do good to those who hate you, bless those who curse you, pray for those who mistreat you."

Oh, I stopped reading for a moment. *I know this one. Everyone knows this one.* I was a little disappointed to have picked such a famous Bible quote. I would have liked it better

102

if it was a verse I was less familiar with. *And this verse doesn't really speak to my heart right now. Because it's not like Maxine is really my enemy or anything. I just find her annoying.* But I kept reading. "If someone slaps you on one cheek, turn to them the other also. If someone takes your coat, do not withhold your shirt from them."

What? I shut the Bible with a stunned snap. The verse had just gone from not meaning anything to me to sounding weirdly specific. Maxine *had* taken my coat! I *had* withheld my shirt from her! Both things had literally happened! *No way,* I thought. *There was no way God is telling me to let her have my coat. It was the last present my mother had given me before she died. There was just no way. And if he wanted me to give her my shirt, why would he have made me think to put my name on my shirt instead?*

I stopped reading. I was afraid that if I kept going, it might tell me to do more things that I didn't want to do or didn't understand. I hugged my knees and stared out over the water.

My mother loved God, I remembered, *and was always teaching me to follow Him. But she also told me to stand up for myself with other people. Can't I follow Jesus but also stand up to Maxine?* I thought, pouting. *It just doesn't make sense that God would want me to hand over my things to a thief and a liar!* I hugged my knees tighter and rested my face against them. The shade, the tree, the water . . . none of them were bringing me peace anymore. In fact, I wasn't feeling peaceful at all, even in that quiet little corner of the world and with the Bible beside me.

A gentle rustling sound made me look up. Sunny stood over me, her dark outline blocking out the sun. "Can I sit here?" she asked.

I nodded. She sat next to me cross-legged style and picked up the Bible. "What verse did you get?"

The slip of paper was still in my hand. I waved it at her. She tilted her head to read it and then began flipping through the pages of the Bible. "Here we are. Ah! This one. Well, what did you think?"

"I stopped reading after the 'shirt' part," I admitted. Then I let it all spill out. How Maxine kept lying all the time, how she took my coat without asking, how she had tried to take my shirt from me, how she'd even taken Misty from me—not to mention Ashton's bed. I took a deep breath of air (after running out of breath from talking so much) and ended with, ". . . and it sounds like God is telling me to just let her have whatever she wants or something. That's just not fair!"

"Hmm," Sunny said. "Is that what God is saying to you? Why don't we read the whole Scripture passage first and then give it some more prayerful thought?" She opened the Bible and read, "Give to everyone who asks you, and if anyone takes what belongs to you, do not demand it back. Do to others as you would have them do to you." She marked the page with her finger. "See? It says 'give to everyone who asks you,'" Sunny said. "And didn't you tell me that Maxine takes without asking?"

I shuddered. "It also says if anyone takes what's yours to not demand it back."

"'Demand' is a strong word," Sunny said. "I'm sure it means you can ask for it back nicely."

I hadn't thought of that. "But what if they don't give it back?"

"Didn't Maxine give you the coat and the shirt back? She didn't try to keep them."

"Because I didn't let her!"

"Maybe. But . . . I think you're missing the point. What Jesus is talking about here is the power of your choice. The choice to be generous. To give more than what is asked or expected of you. God is very generous. When we choose to be charitable, we are choosing to behave like God. Do you know what charity means?"

"Like, giving to the needy? Donating?"

"Yes, it does mean that. But the real translation of the word is "love." Because giving to your neighbor—or fellow person—is how we show love to them. You know that poster in your cabin about love? Well, there's more to that passage. Actually, the Bible's right here! Let's look it up."

Since I knew it was from Paul's first letter to the Corinthians, I knew it would be somewhere after the Gospels in the New Testament. I flipped over to it and found its thirteenth chapter, and handed it back to Sunny. "There," she said, underlining words with her pointer finger. "Read that part."

"Verse thirteen? Okay." I cleared my throat. "And now these three remain: faith, hope and love. But the greatest of these is love."

"God says the best gift to share is love. In some translations the word 'charity' is used instead. Like I said, it means the same thing. Love your neighbor."

"But is God really telling me to give Maxine my coat and shirt?"

"I think he's just telling you to be kind and patient and loving with her. And if she wants to wear your coat, is that really such a bad thing? It is within your power *to choose to let her* wear it. To give her permission to borrow it. How do you think it would make her feel if you let her?"

"She'd probably be thrilled," I said, imagining the looks of disbelief and then joy that would cross her face if that ever happened. Then, to my surprise, my heart suddenly felt warm again, the way it had when I had taken care of the horses. When I had shown them love.

"And I bet she wouldn't feel the need to take it from you if she knew you'd freely lend it to her," Sunny said getting up and brushing her shorts off. "Pray about it. I'm going to chat with another one of your cabinmates."

"Thanks," I said with a wave. As she walked away, I settled back against the rock and closed my eyes. I was feeling a little more peaceful again. "Lord, please show me how to be patient and kind with Maxine," I whispered. "Especially when I don't want to." Then I sat, not moving for the next few minutes, and just listened to the wind as it lightly breezed through the trees, knowing that somehow God would show me what to do.

Chapter 13

That evening at dinner, as we all sat around the table, I had my first inspiration on how to show Maxine some loving kindness. It was when Gio, Kaydence, Ashton, and I were telling the other girls about our horse grooming experiences.

"It was so much fun!" Gio said. "Like we were running a horsey beauty parlor, or something."

"We even got to braid Blessing's mane!" I said. "Trish showed us how to do this cool diamond design pattern thing." I made myself turn toward Maxine and smile at her. "It's easy once you get the hang of it, and it came out so pretty. Maybe you'll get to do something like that tomorrow!"

Maxine didn't look that excited about it. "Oh. Yeah. That would be . . . nice."

"What's the matter?" I asked.

"Nothing. It's just that . . . well, maybe I won't go tomorrow. What will *you* be doing?"

"Taking your place if you don't go! I love horses! I thought you did too."

"I do. I just don't think Misty likes me very much."

"I'm sure she likes you. But you know, if you brush her and give her treats and clean her stall she'll *love* you!"

"You really think so?" There was hope in Maxine's eyes.

"Oh, yeah. Plus it's lots of fun. You'll see."

"Speaking of fun," Gio interrupted. "We're still having our Winter Sisters singalong later, aren't we?"

"I've got the music on my phone back at the cabin!" Kaydence said.

"Maybe we can try dressing up like the characters!" Heaven said.

"I've got the perfect nail polish for that!" Tangie said. "Iridescent Icicle! We can do mani-pedis!"

"And we've got a jewelry making kit with all kinds of beads and stuff," Harmony said. "We can make earrings and bracelets at the party!"

Suddenly we were all chatting and laughing over dinner. I got so involved in making plans for our party that I didn't notice four girls from the Philippians cabin when they got up from their table and made their way to the stage until Aston nudged me. "Look, it's Ansley!"

"What? Oh, yeah!"

Ansley was not shy like me. She was the first of her cabin-mates to hit the stage and she even did a little cartwheel once she was there. (She loved gymnastics and tumbling.) Then she did a little twirl to the microphone and said, "The Flips present: The Parable of the Talents!"

We all applauded.

"I'm Ms. DaBoss," Ansley continued, with a chuckle. "I'm a very wealthy businessperson, who's very good at making money, but I'm about to go out of town. While I'm away I'll need my employees to keep my business going. So I've called three of them into my office."

She strode over to her "desk" (a small folding table) and pushed an imaginary button. "Um, secretary-person? You may send them in now!"

Her three bunkmates stepped forward and lined up before her.

"Here's what I need you to do, folks." Ansley began slapping the back of one hand into the palm of the other. "Make! Me! Some! Money!"

It was funny to see the "employees" all trying not to laugh.

Ansley continued, "But we all know that you need money to make money, so here's what you're gonna do." She started handing out coins to each of them.

To the first girl she said, "Here's three talents. When I come back I wanna see more! Got it?"

"Yes, sir! Um, ma'am. Boss," the first girl said, first saluting and then curtsying.

Ansley dropped some coins into the second girl's outstretched hands. "Here are two for you. It might be less money but I need you to do the same job: that is—Make! Me! Some! Money! Got it?"

"Yes, boss!" the second girl said.

"So, when I come back," Ansley said, "are you going to give me two coins?"

"No, boss!"

"What are you going to give me?"

"Um . . . more?"

"That's right!" Ansley said. She started to pretend she was wearing suspenders as she walked up and down the stage. "Now, you," she said to the third camper.

"Yes, boss?"

"Here's a coin. One talent. It's only one, but I still wanna see more when I come back. You hear me?"

"Yes, boss!"

When Ansley left the stage to go on her "trip," the three employees went to work.

"I'm investing these in some stock!" the first girl said. "It's a bit risky, but if it works, I could double my money!" Then she pulled out three other coins from her pocket. "It worked! It worked! I now have six talents! Wait till the boss gets back. She will be thrilled!"

The second girl said, "I'm going to make a business deal for our company. If this works out, I can double my money!" Then she pulled out another two coins from one of her pockets. "It worked! It worked! Now I have four coins to show my boss!"

The third girl walked up and down the stage wringing her hands. "I only have one coin. If I invest it in a stock that fails, I could lose it all! If I try to make a business deal that doesn't work out, I could lose it that way too! The only thing to do is to keep it safe, so I'll put it in this box and bury it in the ground. That way it'll stay shiny and new and untouched. I'll dig it back up when the boss comes back and she'll see I didn't lose her money."

Ansley did a cartwheel when she returned to the stage. "I'm back at Flip Enterprises," she said. She pressed the invisible button on her "desk" again. "Secretary-person, send my three trusty employees in!"

When the first and second girls showed her that they had doubled the money she had given them, Ansley did a little dance of celebration for each of them. "Great job, guys!" she said. "You did what I asked and gave me back more than I gave you. For that I am rewarding you both with more responsibilities and a raise!"

The first and second girls hugged each other and jumped up and down. "We've been promoted!"

When Ansley called the third girl to her, we in the audience all kind of went, "Uh-oh."

The third girl opened her hand and showed Ansley the coin. "Here you go!" she said in a proud voice. "It's all there! Sure, I didn't make you any money, but I didn't lose the money you gave me, either. Those other two might have lost you a lot. But I wasn't going to take that chance with your money. And see? How nice this coin looks! Because it hasn't been used, it's much shinier than the dirty old coins the others gave you."

Ansley threw up her arms the way she usually did in gymnastics when she stuck a landing. "WHAT?" she yelled out. "Ten dirty coins are worth a lot more than one clean one. Why didn't you do what I told you to do? You failed to obey me!"

"But . . . but . . ." the third girl said, "if I *did* do what you told me to do, I could have lost it all!"

"I would have been happier if you lost it doing what I told you! Instead you disobeyed me!" Ansley said. Then she swiped the coin out of the girl's hand. "Now you've really lost the money! *And* your job! You're fired!"

Then all the actors on the stage froze in place for about five seconds before Ansley turned toward the audience and said in her normal (much sweeter) voice, "The end." And bowed.

As we all applauded, Ms. Cameron joined in and stepped onto the stage. "Good job, girls!" she said, giving the actors a thumbs-up. As they left the stage, all the actors bowed and waved with Ansley giving an extra-special wave to me and Ashton before leaping off.

Ms. Cameron then took the microphone off the stand and

addressed us all. "Some of you may have realized that this is the same story that was the subject of the song that DoveSword sang this afternoon. That's because we would like you all to think about the talents that God has given *you* with which to increase the wealth of his kingdom! To some of you he has given great intelligence, a gift that can be used to advance science, medicine, or the judicial system. To others he has given creative talents. Singing, dancing, art—they all help to make life more enjoyable and worth living. To others he has given more emotional and spiritual gifts, like the ability to listen to others and give them comfort, or the ability to preach or to teach." She paused for a moment, giving us time to think about all the gifts she mentioned. "To some people he has given many talents. To others just a few. But whatever talent or talents God has blessed you with, what truly matters is that you make sure to use them as God would want you to."

When she was done, the cafeteria got immediately noisy as everyone began talking.

Sunny, who had sat down with us just as the skit began, asked, "So, what do you think about what she said?"

Kaydence frowned in thought. "Well, she's not talking about making money for God, is she?"

"You're right. Increasing the wealth of his kingdom doesn't mean making money. It means . . . storing up treasures in Heaven. In his first letter to Timothy, Paul writes that the wealthy one must 'do good, be rich in good works, and generous and ready to share.'"

"But what if you're not wealthy?" Maxine asked. "I don't have things to share."

"Actually, everyone's wealthy," Sunny said. "If we've received Jesus in our lives and we trust God with our lives, then we have the greatest treasure there is! And we can carry it with us all the time. It's a special kind of wealth too. The kind you can keep giving away, but that never runs out. In fact, the more you give, the more it increases. If you give others time, attention, under-standing, compassion, yes, and money, too, to those in need if you can—then you are giving from that wealth and building up the treasures in Heaven. You can share your toys, your books, your clothes, your friends. These are all forms of giving love. And if you love others in this way, then you won't fail to do what God has asked you to do, the way that third person did, sadly, in the skit we just saw."

"Because love never fails!" Ashton sang out.

"Love never fails!" the rest of us echoed. It was the Cori Squad slogan, after all.

Then I got quiet. I needed some time to think about all I had seen and heard that day.

Sunny whispered, "You okay, there, Amber?"

"Yeah," I said. "It's just . . . I think . . . well, I think I *will* read my poem at the cabaret."

Maxine jumped a little just then. *Did she just like, hiccup, or something?* I wondered, flashing her a look. But Maxine didn't meet my eye. She just looked down at her fingernails and began nibbling each one of them, one after the other, the way she had at the barn. I turned back to Sunny. ". . . if there's still room."

"Oh!" Sunny clasped her hands together. "Of course there's still room in the cabaret for you. What made you decide to do it?"

"I know I can sing," I said, "but that's not the only talent I have. I mean, I can write too. And if I should be using all my talents to build treasure in Heaven, then maybe my not reading that poem is kind of like me burying that talent in the ground, isn't it?" I shuddered. "I don't want to do that!"

Sunny nodded. "And if there's anyone else at the table who'd like to read their poems on cabaret night, please let me know."

When it was time to head back, I was feeling pretty good. I was being kind to Maxine and had decided that I was going to recite my poem. Plus, we would soon be having that sing-along in our cabin. I was practically skipping my way back when Maxine made me stop cold. "I don't think you should read your poem at the cabaret," she said. "Your real talent is singing."

By the time I pushed open the door to our cabin I was dragging my feet. The other girls pushed past me to bounce inside and get ready for the singalong, but I wasn't feeling it anymore. A few minutes before, I had been in such a good mood! I had felt like one of those helium balloons that can stay up by themselves, bouncing along in the air. Now I just felt like one that was slowly deflating, losing its shine, and sinking to the floor. And it was all because of what Maxine had said. *But why did she say that?* I couldn't help wondering. *Was she trying to stop me from reading my poem out loud or something? Trying to make me feel bad about my writing? What?* I peeked at her just as she rushed past me, dove onto her bed, and slid the notebook out from under her pillow. I narrowed my eyes. *Now what is she up to?*

"Let's all change into our pajamas first and make this a real slumber party!" Kaydence called out.

"Good idea! I have pajamas with snowflakes on them," Gio said, taking them out of her trunk. "Kinda weird for a summer camp, I know. But they turn out to be just perfect for a Winter Sisters Singalong Slumber Party!"

Heaven started saying it over and over and faster and faster, "Wintersisterssingalongslumberparty! Wintersisterssingalong-slumberparty!"

"Should we brush our teeth?" Harmony asked above all the noise we were making.

"Are you kidding?" Tangie said. "Not yet! I've got snacks! Wait here!" She ran into her room and came back with candy bars and a bag of popcorn. "I went to the snack shack during free time!"

"Oooh!"

"Yummm!"

"Yes!"

"Gimme!"

The way the other girls pounced on her you'd never know they'd just eaten. Some had even had dessert too.

Harmony caught me staring at her as she crammed fistfuls of the cheese flavored popcorn into her mouth. She paused and said to me, "Exercise makes you hungry." As she said this, bits of orangey popcorn flew out of her mouth and down her shirt. We all burst out laughing.

Ashton didn't take part in the craziness. Instead she walked calmly to her room and came back into my room a few minutes later with a bag of yarn and crocheting needles in one hand and her cell phone in the other. "I'm going to work on that granny square while I sing," she announced. "If anyone else wants to make a square for my friend's shawl, let me know! Plus," she waved her phone, "I also want to record some of this to show my family and friends."

Kaydence started mugging for the camera. "Oooh! Film me! Film me!"

"No, me! Me!" Gio playfully shoved Kaydence to the side so that she was in front of the camera. "Besides, don't you need to get the music?"

"That'll take two seconds," Kaydence clucked her tongue but went to get her phone.

More snacks started coming out of people's trunks and all eight of us gathered in my side of the cabin. Ashton climbed up to my bunk and claimed it for her crocheting space. She placed all the yarn and other supplies on my bed and began filming us from there. "This is the perfect spot to fit all of you in," she explained. Then she turned the camera on herself. "Hi, Rani! So here we are at Camp Caracara, and this is the Cori Squad! Say 'hi' everybody!"

We all waved and hooted and said "hello" to Rani.

Tangie began setting up her "nail salon" in one corner of the room, near the head of Gio's bunk. Gio sat on her bunk and dangled her feet so that Tangie could give her a pedicure. "Iridescent Icicle?" Tangie asked.

"But of course!" Gio giggled. "But what's that one you're wearing?"

Tangie flashed her fingers. "Disco Grape."

Ashton, who had heard the name, yelled out, "Disco Grape?" and laughed hard.

"That would make a great band name," Gio said. "If we ever make that band, that's what we should call ourselves!"

Even though I laughed with everyone else, I didn't think I would ever really want to be a in band called "Disco Grape." I mean, I had a silly streak, but really!

During all the jokes and laughing and snacking, I noticed Maxine just sat on her bed, deep inside the bunk with her back against the wall ignoring us as she wrote inside her spiral notebook.

"What are you doing?" I asked her.

"Nothing," she said, turning her pencil upside down to erase something she had just written.

"Come on, Amber! Get into your pjs!" Gio said. "And let's get started!"

We decided to play the whole soundtrack and to sing each song in the order that they played. Sometimes we all sang together, other times we sang solos. Sometimes we played the same song three times in a row so different people could sing the solo. When we got to everyone's favorite, Princess Crystelle's solo, we all started to get up from our places on the floor to belt out the song as loud as we could.

"Wait!" Gio said, holding up a hand. "Amber! You should wear your fluffy jacket when you sing this. It kind of looks like the princess's snow coat! Don't you think?"

"Yeah! That would be perfect!" Kaydence said.

Ashton climbed down the ladder still holding the granny square she was working on with one hand. "I'll go get it," she said, and she walked to her trunk crocheting the whole way. We put the music on pause and waited. And waited. And . . .

"Amber . . . !" Ashton called me from her room.

"What?" Something in the tone of her voice made my heart lurch.

"You'd better get over here!"

I broke away from the party with my heartbeat pounding in my ears and dashed through the bathroom to Ashton's room. I found her on her knees in front of her trunk, surrounded by piles of clothes and sports equipment. She looked up at me with a very serious face. "I can't find it!" she told me. "It's not here. Your jacket! It's gone!"

Chapter 14

I dropped to my knees next to her and began looking through her mostly empty trunk.

"I just did that!" Ashton sighed loudly and rose to her feet.

"I *know* you did," I told her, "but I can't help it. I can't believe it. How can it be missing?" I sprang to my feet and whirled around to look at her. "I thought you were going to keep this locked!"

"I know. I'm sorry. I guess I must have forgotten," Ashton said.

"But where can it be?" I asked. My question was to the wall, the beds, the trunk, and the air. I wished one of them could answer me.

Ashton crossed her arms. "I can give you one guess."

I knew what she was thinking. It had been my first thought too. Maxine must have taken it. But when? And where was it now?

"Sunny?" I called out. "We have a problem."

Sunny came into the room followed by Gio and Kaydence, who wore concerned—and curious—expressions on their faces. "What's going on, ladies?"

When we told Sunny about my missing coat, both Gio and Kaydence exploded. "Maxine! It must have been Maxine!"

Sunny shushed them. "Whoa now. Hold your horses, girls.

Don't go accusing anyone of anything just yet. Let's just look at the facts, first. How long has your jacket been missing?"

"We're not sure. We just found out that it's gone," Ashton said while I paced between the two sets of bunk beds.

"Well, when was the last time you saw it?"

"Last night!" I remembered. "Around this time." Then I glared at my twin. "*When I gave it to Ashton for safe keeping.*"

"So it could have been taken any time between then and now. And you haven't worn it at all?"

"No," I said. "It's too hot to wear outside. And I didn't want to get it all dirty."

Ashton put her hands on her hips. "That's why I told you not to bring it! Who brings a *coat* to a *summer* camp?" she muttered. "And not just a summer camp, but a summer camp in *Texas* where it's like a hundred and fifty billion degrees!"

"Okay, that's not really helping now," Sunny said, giving Ashton a tiny nudge.

Gio tugged on Sunny's elbow. "Come on! You've gotta look through Maxine's trunk!"

Sunny threw her hands up in surrender. "Let's go talk to the others and see what they know."

We all trooped into the next room. The girls were now all standing and staring in our direction with shocked looks on their faces.

"Um, Amber seems to be missing her fluffy white coat," Sunny announced. "Has anyone seen it or can anyone tell us anything about it that maybe we need to know?"

Everyone in the room then turned to stare at Maxine, who was the only one still staring at Sunny. When she realized this,

Maxine's cheeks burned red like she'd just been slapped on both of them. "What? No! I don't know anything."

"Oh, come on, Maxine!" Gio crossed her arms and, because she had cotton balls between her toes, inched her way over to look her right in the eye. "Everyone knows you took it! Now, where is it?"

"I didn't take it!" Maxine burst into tears. "I swear!"

Kaydence jerked her thumb at Maxine as she told Sunny, "She lies all the time. She must be lying now."

Maxine's voice got squeaky and shaky. "I'm not!"

"Look in her trunk, I'm telling you!" Gio insisted.

"I think the fair thing for me to do would be to look in *everybody's* trunk," Sunny said. "Are you all okay with that?"

"Yes!" everyone said. Including, to my surprise, Maxine.

"Let's start with your trunk, Amber," Sunny said. "Maybe it was put back . . . by mistake."

Suddenly my heart leapt with hope. What if Maxine had "borrowed" my jacket without my permission again? What if she then ended up putting it back in my trunk instead of Ashton's? *I will forgive Maxine immediately if that's what happened,* I told myself, and I wrung my hands as I watched Sunny search through my things. As time ticked by, though, it was obvious that it wasn't what had happened at all.

"No," Sunny said with a disappointed sigh. "Okay. It's time for me to start looking through the other trunks. Unless anyone wants to tell me anything . . ."

Again, all eyes landed on Maxine, but she just shook her head without a word and began her fingernail biting ritual: pinky, ring finger, middle finger, pointer, thumb. Pinky, ring finger . . .

Sunny took a deep breath and started going through Maxine's things.

Keeping her eyes glued onto Maxine, Gio stood over Sunny with her arms crossed like a triumphant superhero standing over a defeated villain.

I put out a hand so that Sunny could just hand me the fluffy white coat when she found it. But after a few minutes I put my hand down and Sunny closed the lid of Maxine's trunk with a *thunk.*

"Not there, either," Sunny said. She looked a little surprised herself.

Gio's arms slipped out of their angry pretzel knot. "What? How can that be?" She shook her finger in Maxine's face. "What did you do with it, Maxine?"

"Hey, hey, hey," Sunny said, positioning herself between the girls. "That's enough. Let me see your trunk, Gio."

"Sure," Gio said. Her toes were still turned up so that her nail polish could dry, so she waddled over to her trunk on the heels of her feet. "Here it is."

When Sunny opened the trunk I both hoped that she would find the jacket and that she *wouldn't* find the jacket. I mean, of course I wanted it back as soon as possible. But I was afraid that if she found it in any of the trunks of the other girls that would mean that girl was, well, a thief. *I'm so confused,* I thought, rubbing my stomach, *I don't even know how to feel.* Then I stuck out my tongue. *The only thing I do know right now is that Cheddar popcorn and stress do not mix.*

Sunny ended up going through every trunk, then looked in all the cubby holes, then under the beds, under the blankets, and even inside every shower stall to see if the coat had somehow ended up in any of those places.

When she had looked everywhere we could imagine it possibly being, she held her head between her hands and said in exasperation, "I don't know where else to look! That coat is just nowhere to be found!"

Her words ran through me like an electric shock and I began to tremble. Ashton frowned and grabbed my upper arm as if to steady me. "But where could it have gone?" she demanded to know. "It doesn't make sense. It can't have just disappeared. It's got to be around here, somewhere!"

"Don't worry, we'll find it," Sunny said. "But it'll have to be tomorrow, when its daylight. We can't look anymore tonight. But I'm sure it'll show up somewhere. We'll put the word out. Someone is sure to find it and turn it in. Try not to worry too much."

I couldn't help worrying though. "The coat was from our mom," I told Sunny. "It was the last present she gave me before . . ." I couldn't continue. I sat down on Gio's bunk and Gio sat down next to me and put her arm around me.

"You hear that, girls?" Sunny suddenly boomed. "This jacket is not just a fun fashion accessory. It has emotional value that you can't put a price on. That makes it very precious to Amber *and* to Ashton. So let's be sure we find it by tomorrow. Agreed?"

"Yes!" everyone agreed.

Maxine stepped forward. "I'll help you find your jacket, Amber," she said, wiping one of her wet cheeks with the back of her hand. "I promise. I'll look everywhere tomorrow."

"Yeah," Kaydence told her with a snicker. "Don't forget to look wherever it was you left it!"

Maxine growled at her, "I didn't take it!"

After that, the party was definitely over. We all cleaned up after ourselves in slow motion and we spoke in whispers, if we spoke at all.

Soon we were all getting ready for bed, and when Maxine saw me take the kitty nightlight out of my trunk, she said in a soft voice, "I can plug in your kitty for you."

"No, that's okay," I said. I knew Maxine was trying to be nice since she didn't even *like* having the nightlight on. But I didn't want her—or, even anybody else, actually—touching any of my things. Especially any "kitty" things.

I was almost at the bathroom when Maxine spoke up again. "I'm sorry, Amber."

I froze in my tracks. "Sorry?" I asked without turning around. "For what?"

"You know, that this happened to you. It's so awful."

"Oh," I said. "Um, thanks." I watched as the pearly white cat on the nightlight began to glow. It was a comforting sight that reminded me of home. Suddenly memories of my mom began flooding my mind. Memories like her reading me bedtime stories, or lying by my side in my bed until I fell asleep. Then the image of one of my last memories of her came back very clearly. We were cuddling on the couch. I was wearing the jacket and snuggling up against her as she called me her "lovey-dovey kitty-cat." We had just been acting silly. But it was a memory I loved to play over and over in my mind.

Hot tears began to form in the corners of my eyes. I didn't want anyone to see them, so I wiped them away as fast as I could. And I was relieved when Sunny called out, "Lights out, everyone!" and plunged us all into the dark.

Thanks to my nightlight I could still see the ladder leading up to my bunk. Grabbing hold of its rungs, I began the climb up when Maxine's voice floated over to me from out of the shadows. "I meant what I said, Amber. I'll help you look tomorrow, I promise."

Before I could answer, Gio's voice also came out of the dark, but it went flying toward Maxine like a dart. "Would you stop bothering Amber? Just leave her alone. You're not fooling anyone. We all know you took it. You'd just better give it back to Amber tomorrow or you'll be sorry."

"I didn't do it," Maxine said through what sounded like gritted teeth. Then her voice turned sweet when she asked, "You do believe me, don't you, Amber?"

I didn't know what to say. I wanted to believe her. But I also knew that she took things that didn't belong to her, lied constantly, and pretended to cry when things didn't go her way. I didn't really have a reason to believe her.

Except, I thought as I lay in bed with my eyes wide open, *before, when everyone was accusing her of stealing my coat and she began to cry, her face got wet from actual tears.*

Now the question is, were those real tears for me and for herself because she's innocent? Or were they for herself because she got caught? I sighed deeply and curled up on my side. *I hope I find out by tomorrow!*

Chapter 15

The next morning I woke up with a smile on my face. *Why?* I wondered. *What had I been dreaming?* And when I tried to recall, I instead remembered that my kitty coat was missing. That wiped the smile right off my face. I sighed and got out of bed.

As I walked into the bathroom to brush my teeth, I noticed everyone giving me wide spaces and shooting me weird looks. I was almost afraid to see my reflection in the bathroom mirror in case it turned out that something bizarre had happened to me overnight—like I'd grown another head or a big blue beard as I slept. When I took a peek in the mirror I was relieved to see that nothing like that had happened, and I was, in fact, still the same old Amber. Even so, the others kept treating me like I was somehow different. Like they had to be careful around me because I was made of broken glass that had been glued back together or something. And whenever one of them caught my eye—like in the mirror when we were brushing our teeth—they would give me a quick smile, but say nothing.

Sunny clapped her hands to get our attention. "Come on, girls! Enough of this mournfulness. This is another glorious day the Lord has made. We will rejoice and be glad and trust God to help us find Amber's special jacket. Right?"

"Right!" everyone chorused.

At breakfast, everyone from my cabin tried to be extra nice to me. "Do you want this muffin?" Tangie asked, picking out the biggest chocolate chip muffin she could find and dropping it on my plate. "It's still warm! What about this bacon? It's still sizzling!"

Sunny told the camp director about my missing jacket, and an announcement was made over the loudspeaker that anyone who had seen a white, fluffy, fake fur jacket was to turn it in to headquarters right away, as it belonged to a camper in the Corinthians cabin and was very precious to her.

A minute later I looked up from my plate to see Ansley standing next to me. "Was that announcement about you? Did you bring your kitty coat?" she asked, her eyes wide.

"Yeah," I admitted.

"What happened? How did it go missing?"

"It got *stolen*," Gio said. She looked straight at Maxine.

"Actually, we don't know," I told Ansley.

"Well, I'm going to find out. When I get back to my table I'm going to tell all the Flips about it so they can keep an eye out for it. You'll see, we'll find it, or my name isn't Nancy Drew!" She struck a dramatic lunging pose.

"Um, your name isn't Nancy Drew," Ashton said bluntly.

Ansley came out of her pose to tsk. "You were supposed to just go with it," she said. "But okay, fine. Or my name isn't Ansley Daniels!" She lunged again.

I laughed, which made Ansley smile—I think because getting me to laugh was probably the real reason why she had been clowning around in the first place. Ansley bounced back into a regular standing position and patted me on the shoulder. "We'll find it. You'll see," she said, and went back to her table.

The first activity that day was a soccer game. Ashton was super-excited because she loves soccer. And I liked it a lot too. But when I saw the field we were supposed to play in, I noticed something awful. It was covered in mud from all the rain we'd had the night before. Washing mud out of my hair would frizz it up terribly and I wanted my braids to still look good by the end of the week. My aunt and sister hadn't spent two hours on my hair so that I could ruin all of their work by day three!

"Can I go back to the cabin real quick to cover my hair?" I asked Sunny.

"Get a cap if you have one," Sunny recommended. She pointed to the baseball cap on top of her head. "I do everything I can to fight the frizz!"

"Okay!" I said.

Luckily the cabin was very close to the soccer field and I didn't have to go far. I was halfway there when I felt like I was not alone. I turned around. Maxine was jogging a few paces behind me.

"You need to go back to the cabin too?" I asked.

"Yeah. I want to protect my hair too."

"Oh," I said. I turned back around and speeded up my pace to make more space between us. I barged into the cabin and entered the bathroom, breathing through flared nostrils. Yes, it was true, Maxine had curly hair that got frizzy. But if it ended up being covered in mud, she could just wash and condition her hair *afterwards* and her hair would be just fine. She didn't have the kind of textured hair that Sunny and I did. She wasn't wearing her hair in a special braided style that needed to be protected, either. She didn't need to follow me or give her hair the same treatment I did. She was just being a copycat!

Since I wasn't in a swimsuit, I didn't want to step in the shower, and I decided to take care of my hair at the sink instead. Maxine stood at the sink beside me and waited.

"Don't you have any conditioner of your own?" I asked.

"No," Maxine said. "I didn't bring any."

I huffed. "You know, you don't even really need—" I stopped myself when I felt a nudge from my heart. *What had that Scripture said? Give to anyone that asks?*

My brain snapped back, *Yeah, but this girl just takes and takes. And she doesn't even need to do this to her hair! Worst of all, she probably stole your jacket, and you'll never see it again!*

But . . . what would Jesus want you to do? my heart said calmly.

I know . . . he'd want me to give her some conditioner, my brain answered reluctantly.

Even if she's a thief? my heart continued.

My brain said nothing.

So my heart answered itself. *Yes. Even if she's a thief.*

Out loud I said, "Okay, Maxine, but you used too much last time. And you didn't do it right. Now, I think you should just wash and condition your hair later this afternoon instead. But since you're here, just do what I do. First, soak your head."

Maxine watched me do it first and followed me step-by-step.

"Next, add the conditioner. But you used too much last time. Put out your hand." I squeezed a small amount of the creamy, coconut-scented hair product into the palm of her hand. "Now spread it all around so that it covers the whole head. Right. Like that. Good. Okay, now we're good to go. Oh, but first . . ." I went into my trunk and grabbed a couple of baseball caps. "Want one?"

When we got back to the soccer field, Sunny called me over. "Everything okay?"

"Yeah, everything's fine," I said.

Sunny watched as Maxine took her place in front of the goal. "So did she admit to anything? Does she have your jacket?"

"She didn't say anything like that." I shrugged. "I don't know if she took it."

Sunny jumped back a little. "Everyone else seems to be sure she did. *Very* sure."

"I know," I said. "But I'm not anymore."

Sunny nodded, and then she shooed me away so she wouldn't blow her whistle in my ear. Then, tossing me the soccer ball, she yelled, "Let's begin!"

It felt really good to run and fall and roll and kick. I had been feeling all wound up since the night before, and playing soccer helped me feel much lighter and happier than I'd felt since finding out my coat was missing.

Sunny put me and Maxine on opposing teams. Maxine was their goalie, and Ashton was mine. As we played, I couldn't help noticing that Gio and Heaven, who were on my team, kept laughing harder and harder with each time Maxine slipped in the mud, fell on the ground, and got splattered. Also, they seemed to be aiming *for* Maxine instead of for the inside of the goal. But because they were more interested in hitting her with the ball than they were with wanting to score points, they ended up helping her team win the game.

When it was over, Ashton slapped her forehead with frustration. "Guys! Don't you know how soccer works?" she yelled at them. "It's like you were playing for the other side!"

And while Maxine jumped up and down with excitement

at her team's victory, shouting, "That's right! I'm the greatest! That's my name! I'm the greatest!" the other girls on her team, Harmony, Tangie, and Kaydence, left the field looking downcast and apologetic.

"Sorry," Tangie told me. "We didn't want her to win."

Our next activity was rock climbing. It was one of my favorite camp activities besides horseback riding and singing, of course. There was something about wearing the harness and the way I had to use my muscles to haul myself up the wall that, well, kind of made me feel like a superhero.

The wall was set up outside and was really wide and tall so a bunch of us campers could all use it at once. It was made of wood, and covered in colorful fake rocks that were bolted onto it to use as hand grips or places to put your feet. There were mats on the ground below to cushion us if we should fall, but we also had to wear harnesses, so that if we slipped, we would just swing safely above the ground *instead* of falling. I liked the swinging part too. And getting strapped into the harness made me feel even more adventurous.

As our instructors adjusted our belts, they explained how, since everyone was built differently, they had to make sure the belts sat in the right place (above our hips) and securely because they didn't want any of us falling out of the harness. When Maxine heard that, she began to panic.

"I'm going to fall out of the harness?" she asked, gripping hard on the arm of our coach, Counselor Jack.

"No, this is so that you *don't* fall out," Jack said. He was so muscular that he looked like he had been climbing rocks since he could crawl. "We work very hard to keep you safe here at Camp Caracara. Besides, see? Look how the other kids are doing it. If you slip, you won't actually fall, you'll just swing in the air a little bit. Then you can go back to climbing the wall."

"But if I *do* slip out of the harness, I *will* fall!" Maxine's voice was high and her breaths were short.

"We have this nice cushiony mat that's *fun* to land on," Jack told her. "But you *won't* fall. I promise you."

Uh-oh, I thought. Maxine looked like she was going to rip the belt off, jump out of the leg holes, and just run away. But when she saw me all belted in and ready to go, she asked, "Aren't you scared?"

I shrugged. "More like excited."

"You actually *like* rock climbing?"

"I love it!"

Maxine sighed and looked up at the wall for a long minute.

Kaydence, who was on Maxine's other side, said, "Oh, look, the copycat's a scaredy-cat."

I frowned at her. Maxine might have taken my coat, but it didn't make it okay to make fun of her for being scared.

Finally, we began climbing. Our coaches shouted out encouragement, telling us to take our time, advising us which "stones" we might want to try to grip next, and saying things like, "Woohoo! You can do it!"

Maxine was moving very slowly. She reminded me of a video I'd seen of a sloth climbing up a tree in the Amazon rainforest. *Of course, if she had claws like a sloth, climbing would be a cinch for her,* I thought. I actually made it to the top of the wall and was half of the way down again when I found Maxine nearly halfway up the wall. Only she looked frozen in place. And when I took a closer look at her, I noticed that her forehead was resting against the wall and her eyes were closed.

"You can do it, Maxine! You're doing great so far!" Coach Jack told her. "You're already almost halfway up!"

Maxine moaned.

That wasn't what she wanted to hear, I realized. *She's scared to be so high up.*

Someone on my other side slipped and shrieked in her surprise, making Maxine cringe.

"I'm stuck!" Maxine wailed. It looked like she couldn't make herself move any further up and didn't want to try starting her way down.

"You're not stuck, honey," Jack shouted up at her. "You can just let go and we'll let you down nice and easy. Or you can rappel your way down like we showed you all earlier. You'll be perfectly safe."

"Let go? I'm not letting go!" Maxine scoffed.

Kaydence dangled near Maxine and laughed at her. "Why don't you try fake crying as usual?"

Maxine couldn't even turn her head to look at her. She just kept her eyes closed and sniffled.

Shooting Kaydence a look that I hoped said "be quiet!" I swung myself over to Maxine's side and put an arm around her. Her eyes flew open.

"You might find the swinging part more fun than the climbing part," I told her. "Watch!" I swung back and forth and then landed near her again. "It's kind of like being Spider-Man."

Maxine said nothing, but her arms were shaking because she was holding on to the "stones" so tightly. Plus, she looked exhausted, and a little like she wanted to throw up.

"Look, if I hold onto you, will you let go? We can go down together." I looked over at Coach Jack who nodded.

"I'm afraid," Maxine whispered.

"I know. But wait, you'll see. We'll land on our feet like superheroes. It's going to be really cool."

"My arms ache."

"Let's just go down and you won't have to do this anymore," I said. I put my arm around her again. "Are you ready?"

Maxine thought about it for a few minutes before finally giving me the teensiest of nods. Then she let go, let out a little scream, and found herself dangling lazily in mid-air. "Oh," she said, with a giggle.

"Come on," I said, "let's go down."

Once we made our soft landing on the mat, Maxine peeled off her harness as soon as she could and backed away from the wall. "I never want to do that, again!" Then, bursting into real, wet tears again, she ran over to Sunny.

Kaydence and Gio landed near me on the mat and watched Maxine cry.

Gio snickered. "Please. And the Oscar goes to . . . Maxine for another sickening performance."

Kaydence laughed and used a whimpering voice to make fun of Maxine, "I'm so skeered! I'm gonna fall!"

Gio laughed too.

Suddenly a volcano rose from within me and I turned on both of them. "Will you two *stop*?" I shouted at them. And for once even though I was upset, my voice came out sharp and clear and strong. "You're both being so *mean*! Just stop it!"

Chapter 16

Kaydence and Gio were stunned into silence for a moment. Then Kaydence said, "But you know she's faking!"

"No! When she's faking she doesn't cry real tears. She was *afraid*, Kaydence. For real. How would you like it if you were really afraid of something and I just laughed at you—to your face?"

Gio put her hands on her hips. "But it's not the same thing! You're *friends* with Kaydence. Kaydence isn't friends with Maxine!"

"Not being friends with someone doesn't make it okay to laugh at them when they're afraid!" I pointed out.

"But she stole your jacket!" Gio insisted. "She doesn't deserve us being nice to her. You most of all!"

"But I wasn't being *nice* to her!" I shouted. "I was just being *patient*," I said, only realizing it as I said it. ". . . and kind."

At the sound of the familiar words, Kaydence and Gio hung their heads.

Suddenly the voice of Counselor Jack brought us back to the present. "Are you girls climbing or what?" he called out to the three of us. We were all still in our harnesses, but just standing at the base of the wall when we should have been scaling it.

"Yes!" we answered guiltily, and we bumped into each other as we scrambled to get back to our places at, and up, the wall.

Singing class was next. When we arrived at the D.A.V.I.D. cabin, all the chairs we had before were gone. Or least, they were stacked into towers and shoved up against the walls.

"This is . . . different," Tangie said, raising her eyebrows with interest.

When Robert and Sharon showed up on the stage, they called a group of older kids who were wearing matching aqua-colored T-shirts to join them on stage.

"How many of you remember the songs from yesterday?" Sharon asked.

Most of us raised our hands.

"Some of you out there don't seem too sure," she said, shading her eyes as if she was looking far into the distance on a sunny day. "Well, as a little review for you—with a twist—may I introduce to you the Thessalonian Rangers!"

Robert started up the music to one of the songs from the day before and the lyrics popped up on the large screen once again. And as we started to sing, "Praise the Lord, O my soul . . ." the Thessalonian Rangers suddenly broke out into a joyful synchronized dance.

Ashton gasped and pushed herself to the front to get a better look.

The moves included a lot of jumping and hand gestures. It made the dancers look very enthusiastic but in a coordinated way. In other words, it looked really awesome. So even though the audience didn't know the moves, it got us all jumping and dancing too.

When the song was over, we all clapped for each other.

"Thank you, Thessalonian Rangers," Sharon said, walking to the front of the stage. "And yes, this is a dance you will all learn, so that on our cabaret night the whole room can be on their feet dancing while we sing praises to God! It will be our big finale!"

Kids around the room hopped up and down (we hadn't really stopped even though the song was over) and whooped with anticipation.

I, on the other hand, suddenly remembered what Maxine had said about me being in the cabaret. How she told me she didn't think I should read my poem. And how she kept acting all secretive about her notebook. These were things that had bothered me the day before, but that I'd forgotten about ever since my coat went missing.

Oh, boy, I thought, crossing my arms and drumming my fingers on my biceps. *I can't wait for free time. Because when all the other girls are at the barn, I'll be practicing reading my poem over and over until I've got it memorized. If God wants me to perform it at the cabaret, then I'm not going to let Maxine stop me!*

Even though the dance had been a lot of fun, it was great to sit down at lunch time. All of our morning activities had been very physical, without any real rest. So by the time we Cories got to our table, we all threw ourselves down into our chairs and groaned.

"We sound like my granddad!" Tangie said with a giggle.

"Where's Sunny?" I craned my neck to see if I could spot her in the crowd. I hoped she had some news about my jacket.

"There she is," Ashton said. "Talking to the director."

"Do you think they found your jacket?" Harmony asked.

"Maybe."

When Sunny made her way back to join us, I noticed that she was empty-handed, but I still hoped that she had at least heard that my jacket had been found. But when she got to the table, she shook her head. "Sorry. No news yet."

When Ansley ran over to the table a little while later, my hopes were raised again. She looked so excited! But it turned out it was only to tell me that she had her whole cabin helping her search for my coat. Which was really nice, I'll admit, but not what I wanted to hear.

"She looked so psyched, I thought she'd found it," I told Ashton once Ansley left us.

Ashton shrugged. "Ansley always looks really psyched. She's pretty much psyched about everything."

I sighed. "I guess."

When lunch was over and free time finally began, I made sure that Maxine, Heaven, Harmony, and Tangie were all at the barn before I went back to the cabin with Gio, Kaydence, and Ashton. When I told them that I planned to use the free time to learn my poem, they were all disappointed.

"Why don't you come hang out with us, instead?" Gio asked. "You can always practice your poem tonight. Meanwhile, the sun is out," she gestured toward the window, "and we were thinking about going to the snack shack or the game room or something."

"Yeah," Kaydence, who was putting her hair up in a ponytail, chimed in. "Ashton is going to film us and everything. Maybe we'll film an action movie outside or something like that too. It'll be fun."

It *did* sound like fun, but I shook my head. "That's okay," I said. "I really need to do this."

"Come on, guys," Ashton said, leading them away. "I think she wants to be alone."

Once they were gone I pulled my poem out of my trunk, stood in the middle of the room, and read it aloud:

I am fearfully and wonderfully made.
I hear music and have to sing.
I wonder where it will take me,
I hope to be on Broadway one day.
I dream of being on the stage.
I am God's girl.
I see the many gifts God has given me.
I touch them one by one and give thanks.
I feel grateful for all of them.
I want God to know this.
I am made from Love.
I try to be gentle and kind.
I worry that I am not always.
I pray for help to do better.
I know God is always with me.
I am made in the image of I Am.

When I was done, I held the poem to my heart. I really liked it. It was about God, it was about me, *and* it was about the love we had for each other. But the idea of reading it out loud to a roomful of people still made me feel nervous. "I . . . can't . . ." I decided, and I folded it up and opened my trunk to stuff it back in the side pocket. But when I opened my trunk I realized that what I was doing was a lot like burying it in the dirt—the way that worker had buried his talent in the skit we saw. So, with a big sigh, I slammed down the lid and squeezed my eyes shut.

"Okay, God," I whispered to Him, "if you'd really like me to recite this poem at the cabaret, help me to memorize it so that I don't mess it up in front of everyone!"

I began walking up and down the length of cabin, reading the lines, repeating them, and reading them again. I memorized one line at a time, then two lines together, then three and four.

At one point I sat down on Maxine's bed to look over the whole poem once again when I saw something from just out of the corner of my eye. It was a little wire circle—a ring from her spiral notebook that was sticking out just the teensiest bit from under her pillow.

What had she been writing in that, anyway? I wondered. I gave the pillow my best hypnotic stare, as if I could convince it to slide the notebook out from under itself and hand it over to me to read. But of course, nothing happened. The pillow and the notebook both stayed where they were.

Should I peek? I asked myself. *No! Of course not! That would be wrong. It's her private business. Just get up and walk away!* But I didn't get up, I stayed sitting and turned back to my poem. When I opened my mouth to start reciting it again, the words seemed to get all blurry on the page. And I immediately returned to thinking about the notebook that was lying just inches away from me.

Would it be so terrible to just look for thirty seconds? I asked myself. *Of course it wouldn't. I mean, that's not even a minute!* And my hand, which was leaning on the mattress, began to crawl across the bedcovers like some kind of spider. But I snatched it back. *No! What if it turns out to be a diary or something? Then it would be extra-bad of me to read it! You wouldn't want anyone reading your diary, would you?* The idea made my stomach turn. *Yuck. Of course not.*

I forced myself to stand up. And I was just about to walk away when I had a new thought. *What if it is Maxine's diary? And what if she wrote about taking the coat and what happened to it?*

"That's it!" I said aloud. Then, with my heart pounding, I threw my poem onto my bed, grabbed the notebook out from under the pillow, flipped to the first page, and began to read:

> I am fearfully and wonderfully made.
> I hear music and have to sing.
> I wonder where it will take me.
> I hope to be on Broadway one day.
> I dream of being on the stage . . .

What? Wait a minute! This is my poem! Every line of it! In her *notebook*! I picked up the sheet of paper with my handwriting on it and compared them side-by-side. She had copied it down, word for word! *I can't believe it! The copykitty has struck again!*

I was so shocked and angry by what I saw that I didn't notice the sound of footsteps approaching the door until the door itself popped open. I threw the notebook onto the bed, but it was too late. Maxine stood in the doorway, her mouth open as she looked from my hand to the book on top of the covers. "Were you looking through my notebook?"

I wasn't going to lie about it. "Yes," I admitted, even though it made me feel sick to my stomach to say so. To do something so wrong—and to be caught doing it! I felt so ashamed. That is, until I remembered what I'd just seen in the notebook. Then my shame changed back to anger.

"Why did you write my poem in there?"

Maxine sat on her bed, picked up her notebook, and clucked her tongue. "Now you've ruined my surprise."

"What surprise?" I asked, feeling very confused. "That you copied my poem? Actually, that's not really surprising." I sat down on Gio's bed so that we sat facing each other. "You copied my shirt, you copied my hair conditioning . . ." I had to say it, "Everybody's calling you a copycat. More like a copy*kitty*, actually."

Maxine didn't even deny it. "I want to be like you," she said. "That's all."

"What? Why?"

Maxine shrugged. "Everybody likes you. You're nice. People want to be your friend. You're interesting. I'm not interesting."

"Of course you're interesting, Maxine!" I said automatically. Then I had to think about whether I really meant it or not. "That is, I bet you would be interesting to people if they got to know you."

"But nobody wants to get to know me. That's the problem. Nobody wants to be my friend. You see how all the other girls treat me. They're mean, they laugh. They all hate me!"

"They don't *hate* you," I said. "Nobody hates you. But they don't *like* . . . well, the way you lie."

"I don't lie," Maxine said.

My shoulders sagged. "Isn't *that* a lie?"

Maxine squirmed a little. "They're not really lies, they're more like . . . stories. You know, the truth—with a twist. So that I sound more interesting."

145

"People don't think lies makes you sound more interesting," I said shaking my head strongly. "They just think they make you a liar."

"But they're not lies!"

"Okay, so you live in a mansion?" I crossed my arms.

"Well, my mom and I call it 'the mansion.' But . . . it's a trailer. But that's its real name! My mom painted the actual words 'The Mansion' right on the side of it."

I laughed. "Did she really? That's kind of cool. I'd like to see it someday! See? Your *real* story is a lot more interesting than your fake one."

"You're just saying that!"

"No, I'm not. Okay, so what about all those horses you said you have?"

"I do have them . . . hanging over my bed. They're pictures I've gotten from the internet. I've named them all and I like to imagine riding them and taking care of them."

"Ooh, I like that idea!" I said, got off the bed, and sat cross-legged on the floor in front of her. "Maybe *I* should find pictures of pretty horses on the web and create a 'fantasy stable' of my own . . ." Then I slapped my forehead. "But then that would mean *I* was copying *you*!"

Maxine laughed that time and sat on the floor too. "I won't mind. My pretend horses are a lot less scary than real ones. A lot easier to ride too."

"It was your first time on a real horse, wasn't it?"

Maxine nodded.

"You came back early from the barn too. Why? Were you scared to wash the horses?"

"A little. I got to help with one, but that was enough for me for now."

"Okay, so what about your canopy bed? Do you really have one, or do you have a more interesting real-life story about that too?"

"Actually, I do. My mom and I sleep on this red fold-out thing. We use it as a couch in the living room during the day. But at night we open it up and it becomes our queen-sized bed. Plus, my mom hung all of this mosquito netting from the ceiling. When we take it down at night it makes our bed look just like a big, luxurious canopy!"

"Sounds pretty! So, is your mom like, very handy?"

"Oh, yes! My father isn't around so she has to do everything. That's why I said I had servants! She's always saying that she's my driver, my maid, my cook, and so on."

I sighed. "You're so lucky you still have your mom, though." I gave her a smile, but I felt it quiver on the edges. "I miss my mom a lot sometimes." Then I remembered why I had woken up smiling! I had had a dream about Mommy! It hadn't been a dream about anything special. She had just been there with me and Dad and all my sisters, just like it used to be . . .

Maxine looked me straight in the eye. "Amber, I didn't take your kitty coat," she said in a very serious voice. "I hope you believe me."

I started to reply when the sounds of happy, cheering voices started to stream in from outside, followed by the sounds of excited chatter. Maxine and I exchanged puzzled glances. Why did it sound so close to the cabin?

KNOCK! KNOCK! KNOCK!

Maxine and I both jumped. Someone was pounding on the door.

Then a familiar—and unexpected—voice called to me from outside. "Amber . . . ? Amber! Are you in there?" It was Ansley. She sounded elated. "We found it! We found your jacket!"

Chapter 17

I ran to the door and yanked it open. There, with a couple of her cabinmates, stood Ansley, and in her arms was a fluffy white ball. She held it out to me. "Ta-da!"

"Ohhhh! Thank God!" I said as I reached for it.

"There's only one little problem—" Ansley warned me.

"What—? Ew!" I turned my jacket over. There were mud stains—both wet and dry—on some of it. "Oh, no! It's ruined!"

"I don't think it's ruined," Ansley said, "In fact, I'm sure Aunt Trinity or Aunt Sam will know how to get rid of those stains, although. . . ." she scraped at one of the stains with her fingernail, ". . . some of this caked-in stuff will probably be a challenge."

"But why is it like this? Where did you find it?" I stepped aside to let everyone in.

"It was elementary, my dear Amber," Ansley said, stroking her chin. "We figured your jacket couldn't have gone far. And although we checked the laundry room first, not to mention places you'd actually been to, like the Upper Room, the pool, and the barn, one of us had the genius idea that it was probably still in this cabin—or very close by."

"It was *not* in this cabin," I assured her. "Sunny looked everywhere!"

"She really did!" Maxine chimed in.

"She may have, she may have," Ansley continued in her play-detective voice. "But did she try looking . . ." she paused for dramatic effect. ". . . *out the window*?"

I rattled my head like there was something loose in there. "What?"

"It looks to me like someone tossed it out the window," Ansley said in her normal Ansley voice. "I don't know why. Were they mad at you? Were they playing with it? Did they want to destroy it? I have no idea."

I shot a look at Maxine to see how she was reacting to this bit of news. She seemed interested in what Ansley was saying, but, I was happy to see, wasn't biting her nails.

"I'll show you which window I mean." Ansley led me through to Ashton's room. "We circled around the outside of this cabin and found it here below this one. See?"

I stuck my head out the window and looked down to where she was pointing. "This is the back of the cabin. There are a lot of bushes out there."

"Exactly," Ansley said. "It basically fell inside of them and onto the ground, where it got kind of dirty. It's a good thing I'm small and flexible, because getting it out wasn't easy!"

We walked back to the front room where my bunk bed was. "Hmmm. So this probably happened sometime yesterday, I'm guessing, when I wasn't around." I snapped my fingers. "Free time. Like now!"

"Makes sense," Ansley agreed. "So who was here around that time?"

"Well, there were at least four people. Tangie, Heaven, Harmony, and of course. . . .

I gestured awkwardly to my left. "Maxine."

"I guess it could have been any one of them," Ansley said. She waved at Maxine. "No offense."

"It might even have been two people," Maxine said. "Like, what if Heaven and Harmony did it together?"

I made a face. "I guess they could have. Only I don't know why they would want to do such a thing!"

"But the coat *was* in a trunk in *their* room," Maxine said.

"Yeah, but . . . to be honest, you were the one who was acting all weird when I came back yesterday."

"I was? Oh! Because of the surprise! But that had nothing to do with the coat," Maxine said.

"What is it, then?"

"You'll see."

I gave Ansley a hug right after giving my jacket one. "Thank you so much for finding my kitty coat!"

"Thank you for giving me a mystery to solve!" Ansley said, clapping her hands. "And I had my very own Bess and George helping me too."

"Actually, make that Bryce and Cantrelle," one of her cab-inmates told me. She had dark eyebrows and long, blond hair down to her waist. I wasn't sure if she was Bryce or Cantrelle, though.

"That's right, we're the ABC Detectives! Get it? Ansley, Bryce, Cantrelle! A . . . B . . . C. We'll come together to solve crimes every summer . . ." And as she led them away, I heard Ansley trying to convince her cabinmates that they were going to form a camp detective agency and run it for one week a year every summer.

I shook my head with a smile. Ashton was right. Ansley could psych herself up about anything! But Ansley had been wrong about one thing: the mystery hadn't really been solved! We still didn't know who had taken the coat or why.

"Wait till the others see," Maxine said. "They're all going to be so happy!"

"Let's go find them and tell them!" I said.

Maxine and I burst out of the cabin, ran down the stairs, and headed in the direction of the snack shack when we caught sight of Ashton, Gio, and Kaydence coming our way.

Ashton stopped in her tracks. "Is that your *coat*?"

"Yes!" I shouted, and I waved it above my head.

"Woo-hoo!" Ashton waved a goody bag from the snack shack over *her* head and started running toward me.

At that same time, Tangie, Heaven, and Harmony were on their way back from barn looking grubby, but pleased with themselves.

Harmony spotted the coat and yelled out in a surprised-sounding voice, "You found it?"

"Uh-huh!"

All eight of us met in a huddle and everyone started putting their hands on my coat, stroking it and petting it like it really was a cat. One that had been lost and was now back home.

"Where did you find it?"

"How did you find it?"

"Oh, look, it's all dirty!"

"Yeah," I said. "I hope it's not ruined."

"Well if it's machine-washable, it'll probably be okay," Maxine said. "But you'll probably have to pretreat the mud stains with something."

"Maybe your mom can give me some advice," I said, picking up a sleeve to inspect the damage. "It looks like it's mostly dirt and mud, but wait. How did *this* get here?" On one of the sleeves there was a tiny stain in a glittery shade of purple. My eyes wandered to Tangie's hand. She was stroking my jacket with her "Disco Grape" nails.

"Tangie!" I gasped. "Was it *you? Did you* take my jacket?"

Maxine pointed at her. "Thief!"

Chapter 18

I'm not a thief!" Tangie burst into tears.

"So how did it happen?" I asked.

"I'm telling you, I didn't steal it! I was just playing with it." She sniffed loudly. "I was reading *The Lion, The Witch and the Wardrobe* and was reading about Narnia and how it was always winter but never Christmas, you know?"

"Go on," Ashton said.

"And I got to the part where Edmund meets the White Witch. When he sees her, she's on this sleigh, all covered in white fur, and suddenly, well, I remembered the jacket. I mean, I knew that Maxine had gotten into trouble for wearing it, but I wasn't planning on wearing it—not at first. I was just going to put it on top of me like the way Jadis had the furs on top of her. Like a blanket. And that's what I did. Then, I got to the part where the brothers and sisters put on some fur coats that they found in the wardrobe—"

"And you wanted to wear a coat too," I said.

Tangie nodded. "I knew you were going to be out for a while, so I wasn't worried that you'd ever find out. Nobody else was in the cabin at the time. I even got to check myself out in the bathroom mirror and I loved how I looked! But then . . ." She sighed at the memory. "I saw my hands against the coat and thought my nails looked all wrong with the coat. They were all short and raggedy, with dirt under them. So I decided to give myself a little manicure. You know, so my hands could be glamorous too. Only I didn't think it through because I began painting my nails while I was still wearing the coat!"

"And then I came back?"

"No. Maxine did first. Although I *thought* it was you for a moment, because she was singing that Winter Sisters song, but when I realized it wasn't you, I began blowing on my nails to make them dry faster. And when I thought that they were finally dry enough, I began to slip the jacket off as slowly and carefully as I could. But then you really *did* come back. And I knew Ashton was with you, and would be coming into the room any second, so I panicked. I ripped the coat off and threw it out the window.

"My plan was to go get it and put it back in the trunk as soon as possible, but I never got the chance. And then, I guess it rained a little or something when we were asleep because, well, you know. You see the mud."

"Why didn't you tell us all of this last night?" I asked.

Tangie's voice got harder to hear. "Because everybody would get upset with me. And I didn't want you to hate me."

"I wouldn't hate you," I said, quickly. "I don't hate anybody." I wasn't exactly thrilled with her, but considering how I hadn't been able to resist the temptation of looking in Maxine's book, I could understand Tangie having a hard time resisting playing with my fluffy jacket. If only I had been there to tell her it was okay, none of this would have happened. "I understand not wanting to get into trouble," I said. "I really do. But, it wasn't very nice of you to stand there and let Maxine take the blame."

"I know." Tangie hung her head. "I'm sorry, Amber. And I'm sorry to you, too, Maxine."

I thought Maxine would be angry at Tangie. Instead, she looked thrilled to be getting an apology from her. "That's okay," she said. "It's all okay now."

"Sorry I'm late, girls!" Sunny yelled out to us as she jogged toward us. "It's time to take you to your next activity! Wait—is that your coat, Amber?"

The eight of us turned to look at Sunny.

"It is, isn't it?" She walked up to us and looked it over. "That's great! Where'd you find it? What happened?"

Tangie, Maxine, and I all started to talk at once, but I spoke more loudly and clearer than anyone else. "That doesn't matter! It's not a big deal! All that matters is that I have my coat back, right, everyone?"

Everyone exchanged glances that meant we all agreed to not discuss what had really happened.

Tangie's eyes shone with thanks and relief.

"Okay . . ." Sunny's eyes bounced around as she looked at all our faces. When she saw this was the way we wanted it, she didn't ask any more questions. "It's kind of dirty," she said. "Do you want me to throw it in the wash for you? It says here 'machine washable.'"

"That would be great!" Although I found handing over the coat a little hard after just getting it back, I really, really wanted it to be cleaned.

"I promise, I'll take good care of it," Sunny said. She folded it over her arm and patted it. "You'll see. I can have it back to you after dinner. It'll look as good as new."

"I have an idea!" I said, "When I get it back, let's have our singalong again. It'll have a happier ending this time!"

"Yeah!" Everyone agreed.

Ashton waved her bag in the air again. "I've got snacks!"

At dinnertime I sat between Tangie and Maxine. We talked about horses, mostly, and I told the girls about Blessing's secret.

"Ooh, now I want to ride him!" Maxine said.

"What about Misty?" I asked, surprised.

"Well, I like them *both*!"

I laughed. "Me too!"

When Tangie went to get her dessert, it gave me a moment to say something to Maxine that I hadn't had the chance to before. "I'm sorry I looked in your notebook," I said.

"That's okay," Maxine said as she twirled some spaghetti onto her fork. "At least you didn't ruin the surprise."

"What surprise are you talking about?" I begged to know.

"Did you look past the first page?"

"Of your notebook? Um . . ." I thought back. "I guess not."

"Good. Then you'll see tonight." Maxine smiled smugly and popped some rolled up noodles into her mouth.

That evening Sunny presented my jacket to me with great fanfare. Well, fanfare she sang. "Ta-tadda-ta-ta-ta-TAAAAAAAAAA! Here you go, as promised!"

I took my coat in my arms and hugged it to myself. It was soft and fluffy and perfectly white. I inspected every inch of it and smiled at Tangie. "All the stains are gone!"

"Party time!" Kaydence hollered and we all got ready to have our singalong again.

The twins brought out their jewelry making kit and a pack of cards and Tangie brought out her nail polish (but she sat far away from me and my coat). "I think I'll set up . . . over here . . ." and Ashton brought out her bags of chips, Gio took out a bag of chocolate kisses, and then the fun began.

Maxine stood up. "I say we start with singing "It's Time" now that Amber's got her coat back."

It *was* our favorite song—and what we were singing when the party ended so badly last time.

"Okay!" Kaydence scrolled on her phone to get the music.

"Let Amber sing this by herself, first," Maxine said.

The other girls were okay with that too. They knew we were all going to sing it a hundred times and take turns having solos, anyway.

I stood up and slipped on my coat. Someone handed me a round hairbrush to use as a microphone and then Maxine put her spiral notebook in my hand.

"Sing that!" she said just as the music started playing out of Kaydence's phone. "Like a psalm song!"

And I began, softly at first:

I am fearfully,
Oh so wonderfully
Made in His image.
I hear music and
I have to sing his praise,
Praise to His name.
I am God's girl . . .

I had to stop. I knew those words! They were my words. "This is my poem! This is from my I AM poem!"

"Yeah, I know," Maxine giggled. "I had to change it a little to make it fit the music."

Kaydence snapped at Maxine. "What did you do? Did you copy Amber again?"

Gio also looked angry. "Did you steal her poem?"

"No! No." Maxine held up her hands. "I did this as a surprise for Amber." She turned to me. "Remember how I told you that I thought you shouldn't read your poem? That I thought you should sing instead? This is what I meant. I took the words you wrote and changed them around a little so that you could sing it to the tune "It's Time," just like we did in Pop Psalms class. Keep singing!"

The other girls scrambled to their feet and looked over their shoulders to take a peek at the lyrics.

"Come on, sing it!" Maxine said.

Kaydence started the music again and this time I started off louder and more confidently until I belted out the song like I was on a Broadway stage.

The other girls applauded and cheered me on. "Yeah, go on, Amber!"

And by the end everyone was singing along to the chorus:

> *I am God's girl . . .*
> *I thank Him for all,*
> *He is always with me . . . !*

When I was done everyone was clapping for me and patting Maxine on the back.

"That was awesome!" Ashton said, her eyes shining.

"You really made the words fit, Maxine!" Kaydence said, looking shocked. "You're kind of a genius!"

Maxine looked stunned. I don't think she had ever had that many compliments in her life.

"I want to sing Amber's song next!" Tangie said, taking my microphone for her turn.

Sunny put her arms around my shoulders and Maxine's. "That was a great collaboration! I'm proud of you two." She turned to me. "Now I know you can be shy, but that was so good . . . It would be great if you could sing that at the cabaret on Friday. Can you? Would you?"

Maxine bit her bottom lip waiting to hear what I would say.

It was still my poem, but also a song! It couldn't be more perfect. "Yes!" I said. "I'll do it."

"Wonderful!" Sunny began making plans. "We can put the lyrics up on the screen, like the karaoke . . . !"

"Can I go next?" Tangie took the notebook out of my hands and Kaydence started the music up again.

"How about we let Maxine go next?" I suggested, gently taking the notebook back. "It's only fair."

"That's okay." Maxine shook her head. "It's not my song, anyway. It's yours."

"I know. But . . . *you're* wonderfully and fearfully made too," I said. "*You're* God's girl, too!"

Maxine blinked with surprise. "I am?"

"You said it!" I pointed out. "And made in the image of I Am too. Here . . ." I took off my jacket and handed it over to her. "Why don't you wear this while you sing it?"

Maxine took the coat from my hands like it was a newborn baby. "Thank you!"

"No problem." I turned to Tangie. "And if you haven't started painting your fingernails or anything, you can wear it next!"

She giggled.

Maxine slipped on the coat and was soon singing, "I am fearfully, Oh, so wonderfully made . . ."

As I watched her sing surrounded by the other girls

161

encouraging her, my chest swelled with a feeling of warmth and peace. Sunny glanced over at me. "You have that big smile on your face again. I guess you're happy!"

I nodded, watching as all the girls joined Kaydence in the chorus. "I am."

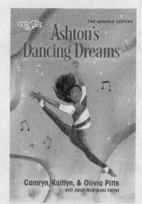

faith*girlz*   *The Daniels Sisters*

Ashton's Dancing Dreams

Camryn, Kaitlyn, and Olivia Pitts with Janel Rodriguez Ferrer

A new city. A new school. New friends. The three Daniels sisters have been slowly rebuilding their lives after their mother's death.

Ansley's the baker. Amber's the performer. Ashton "Cammie" Daniels has fallen in love with dancing. There's nothing she loves better than attending dance class with her two friends, Rani and June. But that joy is in jeopardy when Rani's father announces they may be moving to London.

When she finds out about the school's spring talent show, Ashton thinks if she and her friends enter and dance, Rani's parents will think twice about taking their daughter away from her home and friends and activities.

But her dreams begin to fall apart when the group can't agree on music, costumes, or choreography! Cammie has an important decision to make: stick it out for Rani's sake, go off on her own, or close the curtain for good on her dream to dance.

Available in stores and online!